Berkhout, N.
The mosaic.

PRICE: $18.95

OCT 2018

THE MOSAIC

THE MOSAIC

NINA BERKHOUT

Groundwood Books
House of Anansi Press
Toronto / Berkeley

Quotation from "Wildwood Flower" by A.P. Carter, based on the folksong by Maud Irving, performed by the Carter Family on the Grand Ole Opry show, 1961. Quotation from "True Love Leaves No Traces" by Leonard Cohen, from the album *Death of a Ladies' Man*, Warner Brothers, 1977.

Groundwood Books / House of Anansi Press
groundwoodbooks.com

We acknowledge for their financial support of our publishing program the Canada Council for the Arts, the Ontario Arts Council and the Government of Canada.

Canada Council   Conseil des Arts
for the Arts   du Canada

ONTARIO ARTS COUNCIL
CONSEIL DES ARTS DE L'ONTARIO
an Ontario government agency
un organisme du gouvernement de l'Ontario

With the participation of the Government of Canada | Canadä
Avec la participation du gouvernement du Canada

This is a work of fiction. All of the characters, organizations, places and events portrayed in this novel are either products of the author's imagination or are used fictitiously.

The author gratefully acknowledges the financial support of the City of Ottawa.

Library and Archives Canada Cataloguing in Publication
Berkhout, Nina, author
    The mosaic / Nina Berkhout.
Issued in print and electronic formats.
ISBN 978-1-55498-985-0 (hardcover).—ISBN 978-1-55498-986-7 (HTML).—
ISBN 978-1-55498-987-4 (Kindle)
    I. Title.
PS8553.E688M67 2017   jC813'.6   C2016-908202-4
C2016-908203-2

Jacket design by Michael Solomon
Jacket photograph by Jim Erickson

Groundwood Books is committed to protecting our natural environment. As part of our efforts, the interior of this book is printed on paper that contains 100% post-consumer recycled fibers, is acid-free and is processed chlorine-free.

Printed and bound in Canada

MIX
Paper from
responsible sources
FSC® C016245

for Kaz

The river rises, flows over its banks
and carries us all away, like mayflies
floating downstream: they stare at the sun,
then all at once there is nothing.

— *Epic of Gilgamesh*, Tablet X

1

It happened because I got to school late one morning. Nan and Dad had a fight and it threw my schedule off.

Since Mom left us for New York City, all Dad did was gamble away his earnings. There was no rainy-day fund, and he wasn't setting anything aside for my future education. Nan was mad. I couldn't have cared less since I didn't plan on going to college anyway. My only goal was to get out of Halo.

"You should be ashamed, Emmett," Nan told Dad. "Carrying on in such a manner."

"Lay off, Mom," Dad replied.

"Twyla looks up to you. What kind of example is this?"

"Was Charlotte a better role model?"

"Charlie tried her best. She's not built like us."

"Built to cause drama and bounce. That's Charlie."

"It's been a year. You've been drunk since."

"At least I stuck around."

And on and on. The walls of our bungalow were thin. I heard it all from my room as I pulled my boots on and twisted my hair into double buns.

Afterwards the three of us ate scrambled eggs. Then Dad needed a lift to Reg Voigt's place, from where he'd head out on his next rotation to North Dakota. Deal was, I got to use his truck while he was on the rigs. Fifteen on, six off.

As we pulled up to the Voigts', Reg came barreling out the door, chasing after a diapered Reggie Junior, who'd swallowed a frog.

We held the kid upside down and shook him around for a bit, but no luck.

That's what made me late.

We had to complete forty hours of community service to graduate and it was project-picking day. By the time I got to homeroom the easy options were gone. Car washes for MS, which translated into daylong water fights. Seniors' visits where we could nap and watch TV, or community garden, meaning free produce.

I slid into my seat and scanned the screen: Walk for the Cure (free T-shirts and Gatorade), heart association (heart-shaped junk and sprinkle cookies), personal shopper for the elderly (cash grab), babysitting for young moms (party).

All taken. Only tree planting, highway cleanup and church picnic planning remained.

Then Crystal Jones snatched up tree planting.

My boyfriend Billy sent a text from four rows over. *Running out of choices, Twy. Church?*

Billy Goodwin had only been in Halo two years. He was different from the rest of us. His dad was a businessman from Chicago who'd transferred over to restructure Sunnyside Farms, the largest hog plant between Spokane and Minneapolis. Martin Goodwin was often quoted on matters unrelated to his area of expertise in the *Halo Interceptor*. Locals assumed he knew what he was talking about because he came from somewhere else.

Billy stood out like a unicorn when he got to Hawthorn High. His eyes were the same blue as a flax field in bloom. He wore his sandy hair in a flip, and he had no piercings or tattoos. He didn't care what anyone thought. And he made friends fast, with his Jeep and his money.

While the rest of the guys from Hawthorn spent their free time at the ranges or working out, Billy loved to cook. He wanted to be the new hip Jamie Oliver. Often he brought samples to school. Foods with funny names like "devils on horseback" and "roasted razor clams." I'd gained ten pounds since dating him.

Aside from his delicious appetizers I was drawn to Billy because, unlike the rest of Hawthorn's buzz-cut military wannabes, he had nothing to do with war.

And war was in Halo's marrow.

I decided to go for the roadwork, where I could at least be outside, but Troy Whitman shot his hand up and beat me to it.

Patricia Hooper, our homeroom teacher, tapped the screen and checked off the box beside ditch duties.

"Twyla Jane Lee. Just you left, young lady."

Hooper wore a turquoise wrap dress. She had the prettiest dresses, which she ordered from online boutiques. These outfits were wasted on Halo. Sometimes I imagined her whoring it up at Angstrom, the Air Force base that was attached to our town like a phantom limb.

"If you're not keen on picnic planning there's a newbie here." She pulled some pages from an envelope and leafed through them. "Help a Vet. An armed forces initiative. I haven't had time to enter this one into the system yet."

To my right, Jeremy Colt snickered. He worked out a lot. Under his tight T-shirt and track pants he was all rippling muscle. The back of his head was flat, like he'd been left lying in the same position too long as a baby. Most days he wore a fake gold chain around his neck, with a dollar-sign pendant as big as a hand grenade.

Jeremy's dad was an airman. Following his last mission, when he came home for good, Mrs. Colt bailed. The sergeant went on disability after that. Then Angstrom moved him from the base to a subsidized place in Halo, and Jeremy transferred out of base school and into Hawthorn.

"You wouldn't last a day, Twat," he said, rhythmically kicking his metal desk leg. He reached over and pinched the skin under my arm.

Jolene Bolton got up from her seat behind mine and slapped him in the chest.

"Leave her be, douchebag." She pushed him playfully, snapping her gum. They had a thing.

I'd known Jolene since we were five. She lived with her mom around the corner from our house on Ash Crescent, in a seedy building called Le Paris. We weren't friends but we tolerated each other out of boredom. The only thing alike about us was that we both wanted to get out of Halo.

Jolene's plan was to audition for Disney Channel. She couldn't sing but she was an okay dancer and she could do backflips. She also had cow eyes, high cheekbones and a slight overbite that made her lips puff out.

Hooper made a shushing sound.

"Does anyone here remember Gabe Finch?" she asked. "Hawthorn's own starting quarterback?"

I was still in middle school when Gabriel Finch left Hawthorn. I'd never met him but I'd heard of him.

We'd all heard of him.

Gabriel Finch was a legend. Thanks to him the Buffalos enjoyed a two-year winning streak, which ended abruptly when his kid sister died and he quit playing. The Buffalos hadn't made it to the state championship since.

Framed photos and news clippings still lined the trophy cases of Hawthorn High despite his run-in with the law, which happened not long after he quit the team.

The assault charge for beating up Ted Bruce, a degenerate everyone hated anyway, was dropped when he signed on.

"His mother is requesting assistance through this new program," Hooper said. "The Finches are leaving the country and the poor boy will be on his own on that big farm. He'll need help with the basics. Cooking and cleaning and such."

The Finches lived on a farm that once produced wheat, barley and canola. The property bordered on a stream and had a view of the mountains. But like so many other farms, nothing had sprouted from the soil in years.

"Toilet's too chicken," Jeremy muttered. I waited for Billy to come to my rescue but he was scrolling through his phone.

"Listen up," Hooper told us, her trademark hoops swaying from her ears. "The school board hopes to get a regular-like partnership going. To thank our troops, seeing as many of them settle in Halo after active service."

Our town's existence revolved around the United States Armed Forces. There was Fort Stelan two hundred miles south, where the Marines trained and a lot of our guys and a few girls went if they couldn't get into the Air Force.

Then there was Angstrom Air Force Base, Halo's biggest employer and a city in itself, with schools and grocery stores and a movie theater and a sports arena. It even had its own museum, where vets sat smoking in lawn chairs among old planes.

"This one's an excellent option, Twyla." Hooper lifted a hand with crimson nails to her chest and rubbed the cross that dangled there. She had a chin dimple and thick brown hair she must have spent forever curling every morning.

I looked around the room, hoping someone would swap with me. Even the airmen wannabes turned away. They'd rather clean bathrooms at Angstrom than care-take for an unstable vet, football hero or not.

A lot of the troops who came back from the Middle East were certifiable.

I knew that the armed forces got what they deserved, policing the world and invading countries, killing the innocent along with the terrorists. The thought of waiting on a feeble-minded devil dog fresh from the wars went against my beliefs.

Billy glanced my way with a shake of his head.

I straightened up before answering. "Church picnic planning works better with my schedule at Taco John's."

Hooper's shoulders drooped. She sat back at her desk and flipped the wall screen off so she could have some privacy trolling around on her laptop.

"Whoops. The church slot's only twenty hours. You won't get the same number of credits."

If I didn't graduate I had no hope of a future with Billy, away from Halo. We had big plans involving California, where we'd start our own catering company. Later, Billy would open a restaurant. He'd chosen California because of the celebrity chef network there. Also, he wanted to surf.

I scanned my classmates again. Other than Jolene, who was already saving up for LA, every one of them would get no farther than one state over. University was too expensive for most. Girls on the cheerleading squad like Jennifer, Chastity and Bianca would marry airmen. The twins, Julia and Jake Pritchett, who always looked like they were coming in from tennis, would take over their dad's car dealership. The few with brains would go off to engineering or geology school and return to work in the oil industry, flying back and forth to North Dakota since drilling in Montana had tapped out. Jeremy and his crew would join the Forces or a fracking company. Some of the girls would get in the patch as maids or kitchen crew. If we were lucky we might go as far as the city of Shady Springs for a diploma and come back like Hooper, who'd never set foot out of Montana except for her annual trip to Hawaii with her sisters.

Whoever was left would wind up at the hog plant.

"Coward." Jeremy coughed the word out. He had his enlistment paperwork ready to go. He was raring for it. I gave him the finger under my desk. I hoped he'd die in combat one day.

"Fine," I told Hooper. "Put me down for Help a Vet."

I heard Billy sigh from across the room.

"Smart choice, Twyla." Hooper went over to a whiteboard and licked her marker to get it working. "Such selfless men and women," she added, glancing back toward me. Her eyes glistened. "By the way, you'll need a volunteer buddy on this one. We can't have you going there alone."

Everyone pretended to be busy again. When Billy looked up from his phone I gave him a warning glare.

"I'll go," he said, suppressing a yawn.

The bell went, an electronic beeping like before an explosion. A thin smile formed on Jeremy's face and he flicked me in the temple as he left for the football field.

Hooper handed me the Finches' contact info and consent forms. I went to my locker and called Lucinda Finch between classes.

"When would you like us to start?" I asked.

"Is tomorrow too soon?" Her voice sounded faraway, desperate.

It was only forty hours. Billy and I could cover that in a few weeks, max. No big deal.

2

Five hills overlooked our town like watchtowers. After school Billy and I went to Hill 5, the one with the best view. Up there we could see all of Halo including Angstrom, the train bridge that crossed the Missouri, and Trinity Park. We could even see Halo's official welcome sign on the outskirts. Sometimes kids painted over the name so the sign read Welcome to Hell instead of Halo.

There was no circle of light above our town when it got named. Settlers who sold hay at rock-bottom prices called it Haylow, which eventually got bastardized into Halo.

From Hill 5, Angstrom looked like a Lego city with its identical houses and squares of grass. There was a demerit system there for keeping yards clean, so the lawns and driveways were always immaculate.

When I was too young to understand anything about war, I used to beg Dad to enlist so we could live on base and be part of the neat, orderly setup. Airmen seemed better than the rest of us. They were normal and had rules.

Billy and I sat in the grass and flipped through shots of Malibu on our phones and picked out our top dream rental apartments.

"You didn't say what you're doing for your service hours," I said.

"Cookbook. For nutrition class. Dad got Principal Miller to approve it."

I gave him a shove. "Scammer."

"I'm working on this sweet salmon chili stir-fry," he added. "Total homerun."

I rubbed some mud off my purple cowboy boots.

"They're boots, Twy," Billy said. "They're supposed to get dirty."

Billy thought I adored my boots too much. Dad came home with them not long after Mom moved out. "One thing your mother never understood," he told me, "is if you live in Halo you gotta have yourself a decent pair of shitkickers."

The leather was the color of blueberries. I wore them every day.

I ran a finger along the sprinkle of freckles on Billy's nose. Then he stretched out and pulled me down.

"What ails you, Pocahontas?" he finally asked. He called me that for my dark eyes and hair, which I mostly kept in buns or a braid.

"I'm dreading tomorrow," I told him as I looked for shapes in the clouds.

"He's not our problem. We'll do a few dishes and leave." He lifted my shirt and kissed my stomach.

Two F-16s soared past. The deep, booming sound of their takeoff trailed behind them as they shot through the air. There were always fighter aircraft flying above Halo, doing practice maneuvers. If the sky was quiet it meant something was wrong.

When I got home I found Nan in her Airstream Excella, where she hung out most days. It was an antique from the 1980s, and you drove it like a motorhome rather than towing it behind your car like modern Airstreams. It ran over twenty-five feet long and had its original engine with hardly any miles on it. The generator, lights, plumbing, heating and AC still worked. Nan bought it for next to nothing from Luke Pritchett after it sat in his lot for a year, and she was getting it ready for a pilgrimage to Canada.

Nan was from Alberta and held on to her Canadian citizenship like a crown. She wanted her ashes spread in the Rocky Mountain Foothills, a half-day's drive north.

"If the landscape's the same as Montana, couldn't I save myself the trip and spread you outside of town?" I'd ask to get her going.

She was handy for a seventy-year-old. She'd already patched the Airstream's torn vinyl seats and reupholstered the sofa with a flamingo fabric. She'd drilled blinds on the curved windows. She'd also hammered a contraption together to support a TV in the upper back corner. It weighed as much as a baby Holstein but not once did she ask us for help. Her thin frame was deceptive. She was practically as strong as Dad.

Nan sat at the small table, her silvery hair gathered into a knot secured with pencils. She had slippers on and wore the Slanket that I bought her for Christmas. She practically lived in that thing.

I slid into the booth across from her. The table was covered in blank papers and I folded a sheet into a plane. I could tell she was gearing up to write because she wasn't chatty. I threw the plane and it struck the wall before landing on her slipper.

"What're you working on?" I asked.

"A poem for Len."

Since I could remember, Nan had been writing poems for Leonard Cohen. Every time she finished one she'd tear it up into confetti. On windy days the scraps blew all over our property. There were always bits of paper around the bungalow, sticking to our clothes and feet like Kleenex from the washing machine.

"What's this one called?"

"Land's End."

"Sounds cheery. I need your autograph." I passed her the paperwork.

She looked the form over, her eyes narrowing beneath her arched brows.

"Helping out the Finches, eh?"

"Unfortunately."

"I taught that boy, year before I retired. He was one of the smart ones. Had it hard after the sister."

"I'm volunteering for a warmonger."

She gave a slow headshake. "Twyla Jane Lee. You can be a pacifist without being simplistic. Half these kids sign on to get away from something."

"Yeah. Halo." I knew jobs were scarce. But that still didn't make it right.

I reached for her scribbler but she grabbed it back before I could read a line.

"Haven't you got homework, Twinks?"

I shrugged. I got Bs and Cs without much effort. I didn't try to be anything more than ordinary.

"Never mind. Call your father." She waved me off.

As I left I noticed she'd hung one of Mom's canvases on the wall, all thistle purple and dark blue field and sky. The title was *Twilight's Last Gleaming*. It was Mom's parting gift to me, but at the time I was bent out of shape about her leaving so I threw it in the trash. Nan must have retrieved it.

They had this connection, Nancy and Charlie, probably since neither of them came from Halo. I knew Nan missed her as much as I did, although it wasn't something we discussed.

I left a voicemail with Dad. He'd be at camp by now, resting in a trailer before his night shift. Usually he was sleeping when I checked in. He worked under big stadium lights set up through the extraction site and Nan said his circadian rhythm was screwy, which was why he acted crazy sometimes. When he came home, he couldn't sleep at night but he didn't sleep during daytime either. Or he'd have hibernation-style episodes that lasted up to seventy-two hours.

He used to text photos of the rigs to me and Mom. My favorites were the shots of the derrick. In the darkness it looked like the Eiffel Tower, surrounded by barrels of black gold.

3

The next day after class Billy and I made our way to the Finch property. It took under five minutes to drive from one end of Halo to the other. We'd gone from 17,000 to 7,000 in the past ten years. Locals migrated to the patch and to the wars. And animal disease, bad pesticides and drought had pushed a lot of our farmers and ranchers to file for bankruptcy or retire to Arizona.

What remained of our once-prosperous community? An even bar-to-church ratio and gas stations housing bathroom-sized casinos. The Sip 'n Sea lounge where girls in mermaid tails fluttered underwater behind the bar's glass backdrop. The Graves Motel and Tomahawk Mall. Silk River looking like brown slop.

At the outskirts we passed Ajax Outlets. Only there was the parking lot always full. The Walmart boasted the biggest American flag in Halo, and on windy days it was impressive.

"How'd the sister die?" Billy asked.

"Leukemia."

Our town held fundraisers for Elsie but she died anyway. According to local gossip, Gabriel Finch got into a fight with Ted Bruce a couple of months after the funeral, out front of the Sip 'n Sea. Ted said something stupid, like was Elsie's disease contagious. So Gabriel beat him up, Ted pressed charges, and

Gabriel made a deal with the DA and enlisted. By then practically anyone could join up, even criminals. The running joke was that recruiters and district attorneys waited outside the lounge to cut deals with all our drunk, underage boys.

"How old?" Billy asked.

"Dunno. Six or seven." Gabriel Finch would have been seventeen. He finished out the school year and left right after graduation. Did his basic at Fort Stelan and went off to the wars.

At the highway junction we turned west toward the Rocky Mountain Front, less than an hour away, where the slopes of the mountains met the high plains. On clear days from the low-traffic road all you saw was golden grasses sweeping toward rough peaks in a view that could make the cover of a Harlequin romance. I used to camp and go horseback riding in the shadow of the Front with Mom and Dad, before they lost interest in being a family unit.

We passed fences with bluebird boxes and farmsteads of Angus cattle and tractors drilling winter wheat seeds into dry soil. We passed sugar beets being harvested and fields of drooping sunflowers. We drove by the Hutterite's Honeycomb Colony Ranch, shut down because the bees were gone, then Waylon Smith's place, where Halo's annual What the Hay competition happened and locals made shapes from hay and straw: Lone Rhaynger, Wizard of Straws, Will-Hay Nelson, Baled Eagle, Smokhay the Bear.

From Waylon's we took a dirt road a half mile until we reached the Finch gate, which had a hand-carved sign on it that read, *The Big Open*. The gate was unlatched and fell sideways, its wood posts no longer held by the ground.

As we pulled up to where a barn was sinking in on itself, a German shepherd charged toward us, barking and baring its teeth. Billy wouldn't leave the truck. When I got out, the dog lunged at me, going for my boot as I tried to kick it in the nose.

Billy rolled his window down. "Shoo, fleabag!"

The door to the dilapidated house opened then, and Lucinda Finch came rushing out holding a hammer.

"*Storm*. Get *over* here." She grabbed the dog and snapped a leash attached to a rusty plow onto his collar.

Then she motioned us over with her hammer. "Sorry for that. C'mon in."

She was slim with a long gray-blonde ponytail, and she wore an oversized men's sweater and flare-orange rubber boots. You could tell she'd once been a looker.

We followed her inside, maneuvering our way around towers of cardboard boxes to a mildewy-smelling living room. A crack of light filtered in between thick curtains.

She slapped the hammer into her palm a few more times and gave the room a once-over like she didn't know what she was doing there.

"Drink?"

"Sure," we both said.

When she went into the kitchen we snooped around. Billy inspected the grandfather clock in the corner. He tapped the pendulum to get it going but it only went back and forth briefly before it stopped again. I ran a hand along some dusty shelves, impressed that these people had more books than Nan. I scanned the place for photos, especially of Elsie, but found none.

Storm had stopped barking and the house was quiet. It had the sound of emptiness. The same sound our place had after Mom left.

Billy nudged me. "See a TV anywhere? Think they've got Wi-Fi?"

Lucinda Finch came back with a pitcher of iced tea, poured our drinks, then pulled boxes off the couch and gestured for us to sit. She sat on the coffee table, took some newspaper from the floor, crumpled it and tossed it into a corner.

"Veterans affairs was supposed to offer assistance," she finally said. "But they're underfunded and backlogged, and he didn't score high enough on the risk assessment. Apparently others need help more than him." She inhaled deeply and slowly exhaled. "This lack of resources makes me sick. They should be held accountable. I wanted to sue but Tom says we'd lose. That we'd waste our life fighting them."

She went over to the window, pulled back the curtain and looked out at the dry fields.

"Tom and I need to rethink our future. Tom's got a friend with an alpaca ranch in Peru. Says he could use our help, and even has a guesthouse for us. So we thought we'd check it out. See if we can make a go of it."

She turned to face us again, twisting her hands and blinking. "My son thinks we're giving up too soon. But the pesticides they promised would make our crops grow only poisoned our soil …" She lost her train of thought. "Gabe refuses to come. We're going to give him space. We figure maybe we've been going about this the wrong way."

"Alpacas. Cool," Billy said.

"He was going to go to college," she went on, but it was like she was talking to herself. "Wanted to study economics and classics. The ancient Greeks and all that."

"Are his ailments physical or mental?" Billy asked.

"If you don't mind us asking," I said quickly. "What exactly's wrong with him that you need us?"

She finished her drink and stared into her empty glass. "He can look after himself," she said. "He'll probably get a job soon. I just … I want someone to keep an eye. That's all." She reached for our glasses and stacked them. "He never picks up his phone so I'll have to check in with you regularly. All we need is for you to come by a few times a week to make sure he's okay. Buy some food, settle utility bills, keep the place tidy. He'll be resistant but pay no attention."

Billy and I looked at each other.

"Sure," we both said again.

"Will you be taking Storm on your travels?" Billy asked.

"Storm is Gabe's," she replied. "If you can do two hours, two or three days weekly. Once your hours are up we can reassess. Maybe we'll have VA assistance by then."

It was late September already. Two hours two or three days weekly meant we'd be going until Christmas break.

And where was Gabriel Finch, anyway? It was rude of him not to come and say hello.

"These boxes are going to a storage unit tomorrow," she added absently. "Then we fly out. I don't know how long we'll be gone. Tom doesn't want to come back to Halo."

"Don't blame him," Billy said. I kicked him.

She passed me an envelope. I peered inside and flipped through checks, lists, keys and helpline brochures. It felt like she was handing over her farm, her son and his dog.

"I've stocked the fridge. There's money there for food and miscellaneous expenses. I'll deposit more into your account later. And so you know, he spends most of his time in the decommissioned missile silo. It's nothing to worry about."

Billy perked up. "For real? I thought those were an urban legend."

We were interrupted by Storm's barking. The screen door rattled open and banged shut.

"That you, hon?" Lucinda Finch hesitated. "Come here a minute. I want you to meet some people."

Gabriel Finch's longish hair was fair like his mother's. He was scruffy and less bulky than I'd imagined. Younger looking, too, with dark circles under his eyes. Even so, he had an intense gaze that went straight through me when he gave me a half-second glance.

He dropped a sagging cardboard box at our feet. It was full of bullet casings. Then he pulled a rag from his back pocket and wiped his hands.

"What's up?" He turned to his mother, ignoring us.

"I thought I told you not to bring that stuff inside."

"Needed a new box." He took a flat from a pile, folded it into a box and poured his casings into it.

By now Billy was gawking at Gabriel like he'd never seen a Marine up close before.

"Twyla Lee and Billy Goodwin are going to help out while your father and I are away."

I studied his profile. He had thick, serious eyebrows and his nose was long and straight. Beneath his stubble I noticed a fine scar across his face. It was lighter than the rest of his tanned skin, running from his jaw up his cheek and across the bridge of his nose like a scythe. He also had a large tattoo on his forearm. Markings made up of thin lines and geometric shapes.

"I don't need help, Mom," he said.

Before I could stop him, Billy shot up and maneuvered himself between them.

"Thanks for your service, man," he said, extending an arm.

Shut up, Billy, I thought.

Gabriel stared until Billy dropped his hand and sat back down.

"You're wasting your time," Gabriel told his mother. Then he picked up his box and left, limping slightly as he walked away.

Lucinda Finch rubbed her eyes. "Don't concern yourselves about the brass. He spends hours combing the fields, collecting it. He's been doing it since he got back last year. Keeps him occupied."

"Seems well adjusted," Billy offered. "How long was he over there?"

"Two tours."

I did the math. Deployments lasted at least six months, sometimes longer. If he enlisted at eighteen, then trained and went over at nineteen and did two tours, he was probably no more than twenty-one.

She thanked us over and over again when we left, as if we were there out of our own free will.

"Nice guy," Billy said over Storm's barking as we walked back to the truck. "Real friendly."

He put his arms around my waist and drew me in. I looked into his eyes and prepared for a romantic moment, but something in the fields caught his attention. I followed Billy's gaze. He got into the back of the pickup and pulled me up.

"Is that it?" he asked, pointing at a flat slab of concrete in the distance.

The whole world knew that the government had nukes, but few knew where they were. A lot were in Montana because it was isolated and desolate and ideal for being overlooked.

It also helped that we were one of the least populated states in the country.

Nan said that during the Cold War, in the early sixties, before her time in Halo even, the Pentagon told certain farmers that their land had been selected as a missile site. The farmers didn't have a choice. They were paid to bury warheads in their pastures, and the government urged them to carry on as usual. Anyone with a missile in their field didn't talk about it, and the community was glad about the money and jobs the silos generated, so people didn't complain.

Some of the nukes were later extracted. But there were still hundreds and hundreds of active Intercontinental Ballistic Missiles — ICBMs — lying in ready on high-alert status like sleeping dragons, hidden in plain sight throughout Montana, North Dakota and Wyoming. Angstrom Air Force Base existed, in part, to guard the ones near Halo.

The Minuteman III missiles were classified, hush-hush. Named for their quick launch time, their operational range was over 8,000 miles. They could strike targets on the other side of the world faster than you could have a pizza delivered to your door.

Basically Halo led a double life, looking restful and rural above ground with weapons of mass destruction below.

We were like the loser no one talked to in class, who ended up being Superman. Or the Grim Reaper.

4

I dropped Billy off at his place. His family rented one of the big houses in Affinity, Halo's last new development before the bust. Affinity was a gated community except there was no guard at the booth anymore. Half the houses were unfinished. Windowless, doorless skeleton mansions.

Billy's glass and pastel house shone like a diamond. It had Italian columns footed by cement lions, with an indoor heart-shaped pool. Billy's stepmom was always there taking care of Billy's much younger half siblings. Her name was Cinnamon and she liked shopping for furniture online and doing exercise classes to their theater-sized TV. She hardly ever left, making it impossible for us to make out there.

I took the long route home, past Main Street's old brick buildings with painted ads on their sides, now faded like old photographs. Past Pritchett Motors and Horizons seniors' residence with dark quilts draped on the walkway benches.

Next to Horizons was the low-income housing grid for retired airmen. Men and women stood outside in circles, smoking and drinking coffee, or they sat at picnic tables and played cards.

All the military rejects lived in town. The Triple Ds: Dismissed, Discharged and Depressed, as Nan called them. Last year one of them collected yellow ribbons from front yards and tied them together into a noose, hanging himself from an oak in Trinity Park.

Nan was at the kitchen table when I got home, reading the *Airstream Chronicles*, some draft dodger's blog about his adventures traveling across the country as he blew his life savings.

The kitchen smelled like burnt food. Nan wasn't much of a cook. Sometimes Billy made us trendy dishes like butterflied steak and potted crab with asparagus, which she pretended to enjoy but found too fussy.

It was cold in the bungalow, which meant she'd opened the window to air the place out. The floors under the vinyl creaked as I put the kettle on. I ate the blackened grilled cheese she'd left for me in the frying pan, kicked off my boots and sat down.

"Another day, kiddo?"

"Yep."

Nan set her laptop aside and removed her bifocals. I propped my legs on her lap.

"Did Grandpa Wallace go to the Middle East?" I asked as she rubbed my feet.

My grandfather had been a photojournalist. After the *New York Times* bought his photos his career took off.

Sometimes I thought maybe photography was in my blood. Only I wouldn't trek around combat zones and snap pictures of bodies and rubble like my grandfather did. I'd take food photos for our catering website. And maybe shoot Malibu weddings and parties on the side.

I knew my grandfather had worked in Africa and Latin America. But I didn't recall hearing about the Middle East.

"Last war he covered was the Gulf," Nan told me. "Till then he roamed around as he pleased, photographing whatever he wanted. With the First Gulf War, suddenly you had to be embedded as a journalist and there were strict controls. His pictures there didn't get published. That's when he got disillusioned and retired."

Really our getting stuck in Halo was Nan's fault. She met Wallace Lee in the late sixties, at a peace rally in Washington. Nan was on a road trip with her Canadian girlfriends. She'd been teaching in Alberta, and they'd practically crossed the whole country to protest the Vietnam War.

My grandfather was shooting the rally at the Washington Monument during a heat wave when he saw Nan. He thought she was an apparition in the Lincoln Memorial Reflecting Pool, standing there in a cotton dress, cooling off with her friends and thousands of others. The way Nan told it, he stepped into the water in his shoes and trousers, got down on one knee and proposed.

Nan's friends went back to Alberta without her, and she and Grandpa Wallace eloped to Niagara Falls.

Then a buddy of Grandpa Wallace's offered his bungalow in a small Montana town for next to nothing. A former airman who'd married a Vietnamese woman and was moving to San Jose with her. Nan liked the idea of being close to Alberta and seeing the mountains. But my grandfather left on assignment to Vietnam soon after they moved to Halo. Then he went on to record other wars around the world, while Nan raised Dad and taught English at Hawthorn for forty years.

Some of his conflict-zone shots were online. Marines tormenting civilians, medics carrying dying children through battlefields. Landscapes marked by artillery air strikes, and lines of half-dead prisoners being led by soldiers through jungles.

Nan refused to show me the ones he'd never managed to sell or publish, which no one had copies of but her. I used to scour the house for them on her bingo nights but after years of coming up empty-handed, I figured she'd buried the pictures with my grandfather.

He died of a heart attack before I was born. Dad refused to talk about him. Grandpa Wallace had never been there for him growing up, and he left a lot of debt behind. Mostly credit-card bills from far-flung places. It took Nan fifteen years to pay the creditors back.

"He never loved us," I overheard Dad say once.

"He was troubled, Emmett. He saw a lot," Nan replied.

"He took pictures. It's not like he was a doctor saving lives."

"Those pictures helped end wars."

Dad wouldn't touch my grandfather's cameras so I claimed them. I wasn't any good yet but I practiced a lot. I shot everything in black and white because we still had stocks of his leftover black-and-white film.

I loved the serious weight and feel of the black boxes in my hands so much more than shooting with my flimsy phone. I loved capturing light and shadow, focusing and blurring as I saw fit. And I loved stealing images, holding a place or a person forever.

When I got up to pour our tea, I told Nan about the silo on the Finch property.

She didn't seem surprised. She said that after she and Grandpa Wallace moved here, they'd often see humongous flatbed trucks hauling warhead parts. Halo was bustling back then.

"Lucinda Finch said Gabriel stays holed up in there sometimes," I told her. "Sounds like combat disorder to me."

"Lots are turning them into deluxe places to live out the end of the world," she replied. "Maybe that's what he's doing."

Many of the government-owned Cold War missile sites,

which took billions of dollars to build, were sold off in the eighties and nineties for cheap. Developers remodeled them into End Times bunkers, then sold them to millionaires. Doomsday preppers getting ready for global disasters or the destruction of civilization.

But Gabriel Finch didn't have that crazed look that the preppers had.

There was something else in his eyes. Something that said he had no desire to outlive Armageddon.

5

Two days after our first visit we went back to the Finch property.

Storm pitched a fit as we pulled in. Billy searched through a bag of ingredients he'd packed, to test a recipe while we were there. He retrieved a piece of chicken from a ziplock and tossed it at the dog.

I was fumbling with the keys Lucinda Finch had left when I caught sight of Gabriel tramping through the field toward us.

"Here we go," Billy muttered, putting his arm around me. "As if Cujo weren't bad enough."

Storm panted and gave some yelps as Gabriel Finch petted the dog on the head. He climbed the porch steps and stood in front of Billy, arms crossed and legs spread.

"Hey there, Ace," Billy said. "What are we up to today? Practicing drills?"

I watched Gabriel's chest rise and fall. He stood so close that I could smell him. He smelled like dry prairie sage.

"Get off my property," he told Billy. He didn't look at me.

Billy laughed as his temples twitched. "Sign the forms and we're gone. We don't want to be here either, bro."

I picked up the grocery bags that Billy had dropped on the porch.

"I'll go ahead and take these in," I said.

The boxes were gone. The living room was bare, other than the ratty couch and dinged-up coffee table, left behind with the shelves of books.

Billy followed me in.

"Sign here, Twy," he said, handing me the official Help a Vet forms.

Gabriel had initialed beside each date. He'd given me my forty hours. All I had to do was add my signature to confirm that the information was accurate.

But then I read the fine print, which said there could be spot-checking. Fabrication of facts would result in expulsion from the program and a fail grade.

"Fort Stelan has a copy of this. What if someone comes?" I whispered.

"Nobody's coming," Billy whispered back. "Do you really think they care about this deadbeat?"

I reviewed the program conditions again and when I looked up, Gabriel Finch was standing in the doorframe, staring at me with those penetrating eyes. This time, though, he looked almost curious, a smile forming at the corner of his mouth.

Blood rushed to my ears as I glanced back down at the documents.

"C'mon, Twy. Just sign and we don't have to come back," Billy urged.

"Listen to your boyfriend," Gabriel said. His voice was rough, like there was sand caught in it.

"It's too risky," I pleaded with Billy.

He forced a smile, shoving the papers back into his bag.

"We're staying," he told Gabriel.

"Whatever. Keep out of my way."

"Only if you keep out of ours." But Gabriel was already gone. "What a dick."

"It'll go by fast."

"You owe me," he said, kissing my neck. His breath against my skin made me weak. He started unbuttoning my shirt. But I worried that Gabriel would come back, so I slapped his hand away and skimmed Lucinda Finch's list, which included cleaning the bathrooms and mopping.

At the top of the page she'd written, *CHECK IN W/ G FIRST THING. HANG OUT IF HE LETS YOU. IF NOT, CHORES.*

Billy sighed. I followed him into the kitchen and watched him get his soup started until I got bored.

"I'll see if he needs anything," I told him.

"You're not going out there on your own, Twyla."

"He's not even around. I'll just look for him to cross it off the list and say I did it."

Billy pulled the chain with a silver whistle from under my shirt. "Okay, be that way. But whistle if you need me."

Mom gave me the whistle before she moved away, telling me to use it if I was in danger, and she'd come home. She always made stupid promises like that.

Storm started barking the second I stepped outside. For lack of anything better to do, I got Grandpa Wallace's Leica from the truck and took a few pictures of the dog.

Then I followed the worn path that cut through the field to the silo entrance. I figured I had no choice but to see if he needed anything. I didn't want to fail the program for not following instructions.

The steel service door was locked. I lay down on the concrete circle and looked up at the sky. It was strange to think that under me was the launch facility, a hollow that once contained a warhead more powerful than the atomic bombs they dropped on Japan at the end of the Second World War.

Halo kids got a silo tour in elementary school. I could still remember an Angstrom commander leading us to a site on another farm, explaining to a bunch of eleven-year-olds that there was a live missile stored below the spot we stood on.

The megatons of thermonuclear material under our farms and grasslands were enough to decimate whole populations. Here in Halo we were armed and ready.

We weren't waiting for World War III. We *were* World War III.

You could see some of the silos from the highway. If you came across a chain-link fence topped with barbed wire and a communications pole surrounding a vacant and bleak-looking tract of land, it was an active Minuteman site. Some had long white buildings on them that looked like chicken coops. The second you stopped or approached the fence with its warning sign that deadly force was authorized to protect the perimeter, security forces were on you, assault rifles aimed at your chest. Not even local kids messed around in these places.

But the government didn't care about disarmed sites like the ones on the Finch farm, which was just a shell.

In the last decade, Angstrom offered to implode decommissioned silos. But many farmers did nothing with their empty nuke sites. They just pretended they didn't exist.

When Gabriel Finch emerged from the service door, I rushed to stand.

He wore a gas mask and held a blowtorch. I laughed, maybe because I was nervous, but also because he looked ridiculous.

"Need help?" I asked, suddenly self-conscious.

He pulled the mask onto his forehead and glanced at my camera.

"No pictures," he said. Then he studied me. I didn't flinch. "Go back to the house. You and that clown aren't welcome here."

"What are you doing down there? Prepping for Judgment Day?"

He put his blowtorch and mask down and pulled an MRE — a Meal, Ready to Eat — from the pocket of his cargo pants. He tore the aluminum pouch open with a jackknife and pulled a fork from the knife.

MREs were field rations the military lived on in places where no food camps or cafeterias were set up. I'd sampled them at Hawthorn as a junior, when survivalists gave a talk in the gym. The brown packets had a five-year shelf life, so were also popular with preppers. The food in MREs was worse than dog food. You didn't eat one unless you had to. Meals, Rarely Edible. Meals Rejected by the Enemy. Morale Reducing Elements.

There were some empty crates in the dirt beside us. He turned one upside down and I did the same. He sat and started eating.

Knowing we'd have to deal with this guy for the next three months, I tried to make small talk without focusing on the fact that he'd probably participated in blowing up entire villages.

"Don't you have to add water to that?" I asked. "Your mom stocked the kitchen. And Billy's making chicken and black bean chowder. You're welcome to some."

Gabriel stopped eating and looked at me. The sun lit his blond hair, lightening it almost to gray.

"What's your name again?"

"Twyla Lee."

"Your gran taught me."

"I know. Did you get that over there?" I pointed to my cheek to indicate the scar on his face.

He stiffened. "None of your damn business."

I'd just been trying to make conversation. I stood and start-ed to walk away but then swung back to face him. He got up and took a step back and grinned. I noticed he had dimples.

And then I couldn't help myself.

"What did it feel like, raiding people's homes and killing kids while you were zapping the bad guys, by the way?"

The energy left his face and his eyes went glassy.

"It was great," he finally said, taking a step toward me. "We put grenades in their mouths and made them run. And I'll do the same to you and those shitty-ass boots if you don't leave me the hell alone."

"I hope you never sleep," I shot back before turning abruptly, twisting my ankle in a prairie dog hole on the path. I kept walking, praying he hadn't seen me stumble.

In the farmhouse, Billy was at the stove stirring his soup. When he held his spoon up and had me taste it, for a minute I forgot about the meanness of Gabriel Finch.

"Let's take it with us," I said, putting my arms around his waist, leaning my head on his warm back. "Don't leave any here for that leatherneck."

As we drove away I looked for the miserable Marine in my rearview mirror, but he must have gone back down into his hole. Across the plains a red sun was setting over the Rockies. In the changing light the fields shone like they were bleeding.

6

That night a cold front blasted in like a rocket. It had its own strength. The surges of wind made it feel unnatural. A machine-generated cold burning your skin after a minute of exposure.

Thinking about Gabriel Finch kept me awake. I didn't know how I'd get through volunteering for such a jerk. I considered handing in the forms he'd signed but I'd fail the year if I got busted. I wasn't like Billy. When he messed up, his influential dad could bail him out of anything.

I'd have to come up with evidence that he was plotting something illegal in the old nuke facility and report it to the police. He probably belonged in prison for his war crimes anyway.

At four in the morning I called Mom. It would be 6 a.m. in New York but she was an insomniac.

She answered right away.

"Twyles. What are you doing up?"

"Cold front."

"Take a bath, honey."

"Nan's sleeping."

"Then use the heating blanket."

"You painting?"

"Sketching."

Mom left us to become an artist. It was an idea she got in her head after some bohemian came through town to give a drawing workshop at the community center. She told Mom that she was wasting her life.

The real problem, as I saw it, was that my parents married too young. I promised myself I'd never end up like them.

Mom's people came in from Philadelphia on a pipeline project. She got to Halo in eleventh grade, and by the end of high school she married Dad and her family hightailed it back to Philly. Dad got a rig gig because it paid more and required less training than the military, and Mom got a job as an admin assistant at Sunnyside Farms. They partied for half a decade and had me in their mid-twenties, late in the game by small-town standards.

I never saw my parents as people until my mother left. She told me Halo was a muscular arm choking her. Dad insisted that Halo had nothing to do with it. "One day you'll see, Twyla. You don't need the distractions of a city. All you need's family and big-sky country." He was on his sixth tallboy.

Mom didn't sneak off in the middle of the night. Like a scout performing surveillance, she strategized in advance. First she and Dad decided to separate and Dad moved to the couch. It was hardly a surprise, since they hadn't spoken a sweet word to each other in ages. They invited Nan over and announced it to us both at the same time. Nan congratulated them. Then she took me aside and said we should celebrate, since they'd been so rotten to be around for so long.

For months I watched Mom narrow down her belongings to six suitcases that would fit into her Honda. She'd worked at the hog plant for close to twenty-five years and set enough aside to get started in New York. All the while she told me she'd stay if I needed her. I said I'd be fine. Dad kept telling her to go already, get out of our lives, Charlie. Sure it hurt that she didn't ask me to go with her. But I wouldn't have left Dad.

Not then, anyway, when he was still acting like an adult.

Now I couldn't wait to move.

Dad never clicked with Billy. He assumed I'd attend an in-state college in the fall. Someplace close enough to come home on weekends. I didn't have the guts to tell him about California yet.

At the other end of the line I could hear Mom filling her kettle. She rented an apartment in, of all places, Sunnyside, Queens.

"Your dad cut back?" she asked.

"Nope."

"He loves you a lot."

"Spare me."

"You're right. Sorry."

"Nine months till me and Billy head south."

She took a deep breath. "A lot can happen in nine months. Don't rush it."

"We're not," I said sharply.

"Okay. You should try to sleep."

"Can't. Light's coming."

On sleepless nights when I was little, Mom liked to tell the story about why she'd named me Twyla. I was born in twilight at 4:47 a.m., a week before the summer solstice. If I'd been born in morning proper she'd have named me Dawn.

I remember how she sat beside me in bed, stroking my cheek. She had long licorice hair, a slender body, and skin as pale and smooth as a white rose. A rotating lantern projected stars and planets around my room. She said I was born at the best time. A time where you still had your whole day ahead of you and possibilities you hadn't realized. "You're the light in dark places," she told me.

"How's art school going, Mom?"

The idea had been for her to work days and take painting classes at night.

"I quit. Found a job at a ritzy hotel."

"Why'd you quit?"

"Don't know what I was thinking. Everyone was half my age. Amateurs."

"You mean it was too much work."

"Anyway I have a new plan." She hesitated. "MoMA's got a contest."

"Who?"

"The Museum of Modern Art. Could be my lucky break. Plus there's a huge cash prize."

"How much?"

"A hundred grand. I think I can win this thing, Twyles."

Mom's paintings weren't good. Her horizons were flat and the shading was in the wrong places and her dimensions were always off.

"Maybe have a backup," I told her. "Just in case."

After we hung up I closed my eyes and visualized Billy and me on a beach. I'd never seen the ocean but I imagined it would feel like Montana's endless fields of grain when the wind blew. I pictured us skinny-dipping, sipping fruity drinks and getting all steamy in the sand.

Then my daydream flipped to a scene of Gabriel Finch in the desert, strapped with explosives and guns. I couldn't get the image out of my head so I got up, dressed and combed the knots from my hair before braiding it.

———

On the early-morning news, Nan and I watched farmers bitching about the premature frost. Hunters were complaining, too, about the deer that would freeze to death before they could get to them with their rifles.

Nan needed the truck so I told her I'd walk to school. She insisted I wear my knit cap, which she called a toque. She'd made it herself, a thick purple tea cozy to match my boots, with a dangling pompom. I grabbed it and kissed her goodbye.

Jogging to Hawthorn, I felt my eyelashes freeze over as a gleaming black ground vehicle passed by. Men in uniform stood in the long back compartment and one of them saluted me. His breath evaporated before him, his cheeks flushed. There was this superhuman, shining quality about him in his armored car.

I slid across the icy parking lot to where Jolene leaned against the side of the school, smoking out of the wind.

"How'd it go with soldier boy?" she asked. Jolene had lucked out with her community service hours, entertaining seniors at Horizons. "You ask him about his kills?"

I shook my head. "I think he might have damage from the wars."

"Shocker. Know what I found out?" she went on between drags. "A mercenary's not the same as a missionary. All this time I was like, why are they sending so many priests over there and I figured it was to bury the dead, console families. But then I was confused about the Muslim-Christian thing. Makes sense now."

"Tell me you didn't say this out loud."

"I was surfing the web. Mercenary versus missionary position."

Her pleather jacket cracked as she moved her hand to her mouth. Her dress was so short that I could practically see her crotch. She pulled up her tights and yanked her hem down.

The bell went. She stubbed out her cigarette as I opened the metal door and passed through without waiting for me, even though we had homeroom together. I watched her saunter down the hall, expertly fluffing her blonde mane.

"Jojo's got star written all over her," Jackie Bolton liked to say, patting Jolene's butt. Jolene had her heart set on *Girl Meets World*. An open audition was being held in LA in February, and Jolene and her mom were already coordinating outfits for the trip.

I slowed at the trophy cases. Behind the biggest cups were photos of Gabriel Finch. In one, he stood on a pyramid of football players with a cheering crowd surrounding him. In another, the night of the Buffalos' last state championship victory, there were fireworks going off behind him, lighting him up.

He looked nothing like the person I'd met, who was as cold and dark as the trenches.

7

After class I took Viewpoint Boulevard to walk to the mall. Otherwise known as Screwpoint Boulevard. Couples liked to park along Screwpoint at night. It boasted one of the best views in town because it looked away from Halo.

What you saw from the street were vast plains going on forever like spilled yellow paint, along with a thousand haystacks, the Missouri River and a panorama of the mountains.

I stayed at the lookout a few minutes and texted Billy. Then I headed for my shift at Taco John's, in Montana's most depressing mall.

Tomahawk Mall was located on an important archeological site, a bison jump above Silk River where bones, arrowheads and artifacts were buried. Behind the mall were picnic tables near the cliff. The area was littered with wrappers and broken bottles, and the scavenger gulls made it hard to eat in peace.

Before the mall was built, a Native tribe gathered on the land and held protests. When the mall went up on top of the site anyway, the chief warned town council that Tomahawk would be cursed.

A year later, a new developer came to Halo to construct the complex of box stores close to Angstrom, including Walmart, Dick's Sporting Goods and a Dress Barn. Ajax Outlets took all the military business away from Tomahawk, and soon enough most townspeople shopped there, too. The stores in the mall lowered hourly wages to stay in business, until the staff defected to outlet jobs or to Sunnyside Farms, if they could stomach it.

The Outlets were too far to get to from Ash Crescent when I didn't have Dad's truck. So was Sunnyside, but the hike would have been worth it.

The abattoir paid more than anyone else. A lot of kids at school worked there, including Jeremy, who cleaned floors, and even Jolene, who sat at a desk near the entrance to the hog plant, buzzing people in and out and answering phones. I wanted in, but Mom wouldn't hear of it and for once Dad took her side. My argument that Tomahawk was unhealthier than Sunnyside, with its crappy air circulation and sketchbags, didn't fly. Mom and Dad said if I started at Sunnyside I'd work in the slaughterhouse till I died.

I grabbed my Taco John's uniform from a locker near the washrooms. In the stalls you'd think you were walking on sunflower seeds, only it was empty pill tubes.

Back in the kitchen I ate a burrito and swiped my timecard. My manager Travis Boyd was up front, leaning against the counter and staring across the food court at Carmen Lopez, who managed Arby's.

Travis was in his mid-twenties. He went to Taco John's conventions in Wyoming and he'd had a crush on Carmen since she'd started at the mall in August. They looked like number 10 together, he was so skinny and she was so round.

He'd grown up on a farm, but his parents fell into debt and sold it off. They were heavy smokers and died of lung cancer less than a year apart.

Travis loved animals and dreamed of becoming manager at Petland. We could see it down the way next to Foot Locker.

Kids came out of there with plastic bags filled with water, containing a single fish with a feathery tail.

During slow times we'd sit in the back room and reformulate his resumé. "Horses and cows are great but what about smaller animals? Have you ever cared for a bird or a hamster? Kittens?" Travis hadn't. So one by one he purchased these pets until his apartment was full of them. Rabbits, gerbils, cats and a dozen budgies. He even had exotic reptiles.

Despite his animal farm, Petland kept rejecting Travis's application because Denise, the manager, only hired hot guys.

I put my hairnet on and washed my hands.

"Hey, Trav," I called out.

"Howdy, Twills. How was school?" He was always asking after my education. He couldn't afford college and had tried going to school through military service, but they'd rejected him due to his poor eyesight. "My gecko came today, special order. He's in a terrarium. You have to come see this little fella."

"Are those the ones that change color?"

"Those would be chameleons. He's not eating but he'll come around."

"You ask Carm out yet?" I put on my visor.

"Yeah. Red Lobster then a movie." When he grinned I could see his gums.

Travis's best asset was his deep, buttery voice. He wasn't a half-bad country singer. Sometimes when he thought I wasn't listening, he sang in the back kitchen. I used to encourage him to audition for *The Voice* but he always made up excuses. "Ain't good with audiences," he told me.

That was Halo for you. A town of discarded talents and dead dreams.

———

Lucinda Finch phoned to ask how we were getting on. She said Gabriel wasn't answering her calls. I felt guilty enough to drag Billy out to the farm again on Sunday afternoon. By then the cold air had retreated and a foot of snow had fallen.

When we got there Storm was gone. Inside the house we found a note, a garbage bag and a bullet casing on the kitchen counter. *Clear the field*. The writing on the note was shaky, like an old person's.

"Nice," Billy said. "Bossman wants us to collect his slugs."

Then he came up to me and kissed me behind my ears because he knew it drove me crazy. We made out for a bit on the couch, until he pulled the camera from around my neck and threw it aside like clothes. It bounced from the couch onto the ground.

"Watch it!" I peeled his arms off and grabbed the camera to make sure it wasn't damaged.

"You've gotta get with the times, babe. Turf that clunker for something palm-sized that'll let you take a hundred shots a minute." He reached for my arm and pulled me back toward him so I was standing between his legs. "Something that doesn't get in our way every time we …" He slipped his hand under my shirt and started unbuttoning my jeans, but I pushed back.

"I don't want to take a hundred shots a minute," I told him.

He stood up and pressed against me and brushed my hair aside. "I think someone needs some TLC," he whispered.

I pulled away again. "Do you want your food photos to be like everyone else's? You said I could do it my way. Those digital pictures all look the same."

"Okay, okay. Don't get so sensitive. Least you could do is switch to color."

I put the Leica back around my neck. The moment was ruined.

When Billy lay down on the couch and flipped through cooking shows on his tablet, I went outside to look for brass.

I combed the tall grasses around the path to the silo. I took a few pictures of aluminum cans glinting against the snow, coughing to make noise in case Gabriel was lurking around with his hellhound. But all I heard was the sound of my boots crunching on the frosted ground, and the wind rustling through the prairie, and the shrill *chwirk* of a hawk circling above.

I got as far as the silo's thick steel door, which I tried to open before banging on it with my boot.

"Hellooo?" I called out. "Anyone there?"

The wind changed directions and I thought I heard an echo of Storm's barking.

I threw snowballs at the door. Then I packed snow around the crushed cans and threw those. No one came.

8

The next time I went to the farm I went alone. Billy caught the flu and told me to skip out on the scheduled drop-ins, but I felt responsible to Lucinda Finch.

I didn't know what I was trying to prove. He could have been a whack job preparing to go on a rampage before blowing his brains out. Sure, I needed my volunteer hours. But why risk my life? This vet certainly wasn't worth it.

I took a can of bear spray from the garage.

A leashless Storm greeted me when I pulled up at the barn. The dog barked like he was trained to kill, spit and foam flying. When I got out of the truck he followed, growling at my heels.

"In the wars they plant explosives inside dogs like you," I said, rushing to the house to let myself in, slamming the screen door on the dog.

The sink was full of bowls crusted with milk, the counter covered in boxes of cereal and empty MRE pouches.

I texted Lucinda. *Everything's fine. He's eating well-balanced meals.*

Then I heard a gunshot. And another. I looked out the window and saw Gabriel shooting at a big old oak, Storm at his side.

It was the only tree in the field, a canopy of bare branches.

It stood out on the prairie like one of those Jesus trees in the desert, a hand reaching up to the sky.

I raised my camera and adjusted the lens to the infinity mark, the long-distance setting shaped like a sideways 8. I used the infinity focus to shoot landscapes and stars and anything far. With a wide lens opening, what you wanted to capture stayed sharp only when it stayed distant. The moment you aimed closer, everything got blurry.

I photographed the Marine and his dog.

He was in a hypnotic rhythm of reloading and shooting. But there was no bullseye. The tree itself was the target. Pieces of bark dropped down after the shots, landing around the trunk.

My truck was right there. He knew I was at the house. If he was trying to freak me out, it didn't work. His immature behavior just irritated me.

I went through the rooms, drew the curtains and opened a window to air the place out.

Some tattered books lay on the coffee table beside a full ashtray and an empty bottle of whiskey. Robert Graves and Randall Jarrell. Dreary war poets we'd studied briefly with Hooper. The fact that he read poetry threw me. I expected survival guides, or Maxims and Playboys.

I inspected the top floor. One room was full of gear. Helmets, body armor, backpacks, knee and elbow pads, canteens and sleeping bags. Basic Marine getup, accompanied by a stale locker-room smell.

The next room was empty aside from a dog bed and blanket and chew toys.

The last room was Gabriel's. I pulled the blind back to make sure he was still out in the field. I watched him reloading, his back to me. Then I turned on the light.

It was hard to believe that the military taught order. There were clothes all over the place, and more books. Empties and ashtrays on every surface.

Unopened envelopes from Fort Stelan were stacked on the computer desk. I pulled an ID card out from under the mail and there he was staring at me, shaved and scarless. Armed Forces of the United States, Marine Corps, Finch, Gabriel D., Pay Grade E3, Rank LCPL. The badge had a code thing on it and a decal like you'd see on credit cards. The expiration date had passed.

The screen door clapped shut. I rushed across the hall, locked myself in the bathroom and ran the water. Within seconds I heard Storm growling and scratching, and Gabriel stomping up the stairs.

The bathroom had a lone toothbrush and toothpaste in a cup by the sink. Inside the medicine cabinet there was mouth-wash and pill containers prescribed to Gabriel Finch. *Dexedrine 5 mg Instant Release Take 1 Tablet Twice a Day. Celexa Do Not Exceed 20 mg/day.* I looked these up. The first one was a go-to military pill to stay awake on night-bombing missions. The other one was for panic attacks and depression.

I flushed the toilet and ran the water a little longer before I opened the door a crack.

"Can you control your dog, please?"

Gabriel leaned against the wall with his arms crossed and his eyes closed.

"He's an attack dog," he replied through the barking. "Hard to control."

I grabbed a scrubber from the shower and when I stepped out, Storm lunged at the brush. We wrestled as I tried pulling it from the dog's mouth. Storm wouldn't release it so I moved behind Gabriel, pushing him forward.

It surprised me that he laughed a bit, then.

"*Storm*. Sit. Release," he ordered calmly. Storm dropped the brush and sat panting at Gabriel.

"Would you explain to your mutt that I'm not the enemy?"

"How do I know that?" he asked, turning to face me. "Why are you up here?"

"I was using the washroom."

"There's one off the kitchen." He went into the room full of gear and picked up a camo-green duffel bag. His body almost touched mine as he passed by, and I felt my face redden when he headed downstairs. "Turn my light off next time."

"We should Skype your mom," I said as I followed him.

He dropped the bag at the door and put his coat back on. When he pulled a bone from his pocket and Storm snatched it from him, I noticed a tremor in his hands.

He picked up the bag and opened the door with his hip. Storm bolted ahead.

I struggled to put my boots on and get outside.

"Do you need money? Is that why we're collecting casings?" Our local depot paid for scrap metal, but not much.

As I tried to catch up to him, I could see that slight crookedness in his step again.

"Wait up," I told him.

"All you're doing's clearing the field," he said without looking back.

"How about you stop using this as your landfill and save me the hassle."

"Christ, you're annoying," he said and kept going.

In my mind this was progress. We'd semi-conversed without him killing me. I decided to quit while I was ahead.

I went back to the house and took his rifle, which he'd left leaning against the banister.

Everyone in Halo had a rifle. Dad had taught me how to use one, and in hunter's education at Hawthorn, when we went to a range and shot at clay pigeons, I hadn't missed a single disc.

Gabriel's semi-automatic was heavier than Dad's rifle and it was still loaded. I went outside and walked over to the oak.

He was probably still within earshot and I hoped he was watching so he'd know I wasn't scared of him, although I couldn't see him.

I aimed at the heart of the trunk where there were already so many bullets. When I fired, the recoil jolted my body. I gave in to the shoulder-punch. Then I approached the tree and put my hand on its bark, gray and full of cracks like the skin of an elephant.

For a second I felt guilty for destroying something living. But the feeling passed quickly, and I shot a few more rounds before going home.

9

A chinook wind kept me awake as branches from our linden tree slapped against the bungalow.

I went online. Mom had sent pictures of her painting-in-progress for MoMA. The contest was called America's Next Great Artist. The canvas was a big confusing mess of muddy brownish streaks. She called it *Rebirth*.

In the morning when I opened my curtains I saw that a small portion of the sky was pixelated. Angstrom was doing shield testing again, experimenting with beams that would prevent other countries' nukes from getting in. I used to try photographing sky shields but cameras couldn't pick up the laser barriers the naked eye could sometimes see, depending on the wind and temperature.

Dad had come back from rotation in the middle of the night. I found him in the kitchen frying bacon. He gave me an awkward hug. He had this oily smell that never went away, even after a few days home.

"Since when do you drink coffee?" he asked as I poured myself a cup and sat down.

"Since forever. Can I use the truck tomorrow?" He usually just slept, drank and gambled on his days off anyway.

"S'pose so. I hear you're putting time in at the Finch farm."
He scooped bacon onto my plate. "Billy Bob going with you?"

"It's Billy, Dad."

"Billy Bob going?"

"No. Billy's going, though."

"That boy did two tours. He stable?"

"Doubt it."

"There's a missile on that land."

"It's decommissioned. Rocket's gone."

"Keep your phone on."

"Because you call so often?"

While I crunched on my bacon, Dad took a seat across
from me and gave me a wink. He was always in a good mood
when he first got home.

"Classes shaping up okay so far?" he asked.

"Mhmm. Can I get four hundred bucks for Yellowstone?"

Each year, for three days in midwinter, seniors took a field
trip to the national park. We stayed in a lodge in a town near the
park entrance, and there was snowshoeing and cross-country
skiing. A star-gazing campfire night, and a soak in some hot
springs. The excursion was legendary for its hook-ups.

"Yellowstone's slated to erupt," he replied.

I put my hand out for some cash but all he did was slap it.

"This is no laughing matter, daughter. A supervolcano
means a ten-year volcanic winter with crops and animals dying
off. We're talking extinction."

"Technically the caldera's in Wyoming," I told him.

"Right. State police'll stop the ash from crossing borders."

"Don't forget solar flares and epidemics," I said. "Global
warming and the ice shelf. Nuclear war goes without saying.
And asteroids. Lighten up, Dad." I dumped my plate into the
sink. I missed Billy.

"Wait up." He grabbed my sleeve. "I'll get your cash before I head out again."

I wondered if he even had the money. I'd saved two grand from Taco John's but I needed it for California. Besides, Dad had promised to pay for my extracurriculars.

He ate his bacon and looked off into space for a bit, then pulled his phone from his back pocket.

"We had a grizzly. Check it out." He played the video of a bear no more than ten feet away from the derrick, pacing and snorting. It looked small and malnourished for a grizzly.

"I didn't know there was forest around there," I said.

"There isn't."

"What happened to it?"

"Rangers came. Tranquilized it, tagged it and moved it."

"End of story?"

"For now. If it comes back, they'll kill it."

Heading out into the wind I found a torn scrap of paper blown against the fence.

Our asphalt shingles are crumbling.
Under the lulling snow,
there's nettles.

10

Billy was still sick. I'd been to Affinity with soda crackers and ginger ale, but Cinnamon turned me away at the door.

I didn't mind going to the farm alone. Gabriel Finch could intimidate me all he wanted. No jarhead was going to keep me from graduating.

So I went over after class. Once I hit the highway I could see the chinook's band of cloud bowing over the mountains. The arch was ominous, like something sponsored by End Times.

Looking out at the fields while I drove, I thought about having sex with Billy.

We'd done everything but so far, and Yellowstone would be the perfect place to take our relationship to the next level. Billy and a few of the other rich kids would get single rooms. I'd sneak out of my bunk and we'd have a whole night to ourselves.

I hadn't told Billy I loved him yet. He'd said it to me, on Hill 5 at the end of summer, after vacationing with his family in Chicago. The sun through the clouds looked more like a moon that morning, casting a dull glow on our arms. He said he'd missed me so much he'd realized some things. About how important I was to him and how he needed me. The air was dusty. Grasshoppers landed on the hood of the truck, looking for warmth. *I love you, Twyla.* He'd caught me off guard and all I said back was *Thanks*. But I'd tell him how I felt in Yellowstone.

I could see Gabriel in the field, bending down, standing up, walking a bit, bending then standing again. I focused to infinity and snapped a few pictures of the Rockies. What remained of the snow and ice had evaporated in the wind, and the fields were back to their dying brownish-golds.

I honked. When he turned I forced myself to wave, but he didn't wave back.

The chinook was gaining force and the late afternoon temperature had gone up by ten degrees. I tucked my braid under my hoodie and put my aviators on to stop blowing debris from getting into my eyes. Storm took running jumps at me as I made my way over, but the dog's barking was less hostile. When I got up close I saw that Gabriel was collecting brass.

"Your mom wants you to call her," I said, skipping the small talk. "I get that you don't want me here but I promised I'd convey the message."

Lucinda had phoned twice, her voice tinged with worry because Gabriel wasn't picking up. While we spoke I could hear roosters in the background. She asked if he'd given me any trouble. I told her that we'd done yard work and that her son was charming.

He handed me a garbage bag. "Comb the fields," he ordered.

"Can I ask why?"

"Nope."

Maybe he felt he had to get every last shell out of his fields, like extracting shrapnel from under his skin.

And these weren't just rifle casings our hunters and farmers used. They were casings from ammunition belts and magazines of fully automatics. Anyone from Halo could tell the difference.

Did he miss the military that much?

He must have fired rounds when no one was there with him. There were so many target ranges and Angstrom drills in the area that no local would have thought twice about the sound of machine guns going off in the distance.

"Not much to shoot at out here," I said, kicking up some dirt with my boot. "Why clear the fields if you're not planting?"

Gabriel finally looked at me. His eyes were the color of a streambed, grayish green with gold flecks in them. His veins and muscles bulged when he lifted his box of shells, and I straightened under his gaze.

Then, just as suddenly, he looked away, zeroed in on a piece of gleaming metal and went to pick it up.

We worked without talking. The wind rattled the tall grasses, and once in a while I heard tankers or mammoth Angstrom vehicles passing on the highway.

I wasn't having luck finding casings. He'd probably collected most of them already.

"Can I take pictures?" I finally asked. I raised the camera from around my neck in his direction. I got no reaction, so I focused and took a few shots.

I was zooming in on Gabriel's profile when he turned my way, marched over and whacked the camera from my hand. It dropped on its cord and bounced against my stomach.

"Back off," I said, shoving him.

His eyes widened. "There's no need to get testy."

"I just asked if I could and you didn't say anything."

He pointed to his ear. "Temporary hearing loss. You'll need to speak up."

I was embarrassed not to have recognized it. It was common for those in service to return home half-deaf from explosions and gunfire.

"Okay. So can I take photos, or what?"

"Negative." Then he looked puzzled. "That's not digital?"

He reached for the camera to inspect it, and his fingers brushed my bare arm.

"Do you … mind?" I yanked it away and stepped back.

"You do the developing yourself?"

"Obviously." I didn't tell him that my entire photo education consisted of online tutorials.

He stared at me. "Impressive."

I couldn't tell if he was mocking me or paying me a compliment.

He turned away and scooped some MRE grub from a packet and dumped it on the ground for Storm. The dog sniffed it before eating it, then trudged back toward the house.

Gabriel wasn't talking to me anymore so I walked to the bullet tree. There was a hoard of casings there, both shiny and weathered. The brass jangled together like coins as I threw them into my bag.

I photographed the old oak and thought about the Middle East. Probably it looked a lot like our prairies during a drought. I wondered what Gabriel had seen and done on his tours. How many people he'd killed, and whether he'd been IED'd, mortared, rocketed or sniped at himself.

The bag got heavy fast. I dragged it over to where he was working.

"Why do you shoot at the tree?" I asked.

"It was already dead."

"I'll tell your mom you're fine, then," I said, handing him the bag.

As I turned to leave he cleared his throat.

"I could use your help after all," he told me. He nodded to the bag of shells, indicating that I should bring it along.

———

I felt for the whistle around my neck as he led me to the silo entrance. The door he pulled open was three feet thick. I could go in and never come out. Nobody would hear my cries for help.

I looked at the mountains one last time while Gabriel grunted and dragged the steel door open further. Then he yanked a cord and a single dangling lightbulb went on. I peered over his shoulder into the shadowy space.

"Service tunnel," he told me.

It was reckless of me to trust him. But I had to see what he was doing.

He grabbed a flashlight off one of the cardboard boxes stacked against the walls.

"Is this, like, your green zone against the apocalypse?" I asked, kicking some cases of MREs. Crates of cartridges and brass lined the walls, too. "Or a military recycling initiative?"

"You could call it that," he said.

I put my hand on the thick concrete and followed him down the long service tunnel wide enough for a small vehicle. The air was musty and damp, the sound of dripping water amplified in the passageway.

"How do you breathe in here?" I asked.

"Ventilation system," he replied, sounding impatient.

When I stopped to test my phone, Gabriel looked over his shoulder at me.

"For God's sake," he said. "Yes, you're still connected and yes, we're still on the grid."

"How's that possible?"

"The system was sophisticated in here. I tweaked it and added modems and wireless. And backup power. Generators and a battery bank."

I tested my phone again. It worked.

At the bottom of the ramp was another steel door with a wheel on it that Gabriel turned with effort.

Then he stared straight at me. "Ever seen a dead body?"

I swallowed, my throat dry. I thought about the pill containers in the bathroom.

"Ever wax anyone?" he pressed, louder this time. His voice sounded cold and distant, and his chest, neck and jaw seemed to tighten up. "Ever torch insurgents and watch them burn?"

That's when I chickened out.

"I have to go," I told him, dropping my bag at his feet.

He didn't move. "Suit yourself," he replied.

As I walked back up the slope his words echoed after me.

"That's what I get asked," he yelled. "All the time. Over and over."

I stopped, waiting for more, but he didn't go on.

If what he said was true, it was easy to understand why he lived like such a recluse. And why he got so riled up when I'd asked about his scar.

Then I noticed a path of light at my feet. He was using his flashlight to guide me back up the tunnel.

That's what made me change my mind and turn around: the beam of light coming from Gabriel Finch.

This time I made it all the way down the ramp.

He looked like part of him was still standing in bombed-out districts. But he didn't look like a psychopath.

"You done wasting my time?" he asked.

I nodded.

Once again he turned the wheel on the steel door, and it creaked as he pulled it open.

Passing into the abandoned launch control area was like walking through a science-fiction movie. The room was shaped like a capsule, filled with electronic cabinets and steel machines. Gabriel pulled a square piece of plastic from a slot. I noticed that slight shake in his hand again as he held it out to me.

"Want a floppy disc?" he asked. Then he turned a hand-cranking device down by his feet. "For spare air, in case of emergencies."

I picked up a black phone on the wall but the line was dead. I scanned the dashboard and ran my hand along the rows of cold metal switches.

"Where's the red button?" I asked.

"There's no button. Keys had to be turned. Here and here," he pointed.

"So everyone inside would survive?"

"Someone's got to be alive to launch our missiles."

"But everyone on the outside would die?"

"Pretty much."

Off the control room there was a cot and a small enclosed toilet, sink and shower. It made it hard not to think about the active stations under our plains, where hundreds of airmen lived who were trained to start End Times.

They practiced drills, studied and conducted routine maintenance while they waited. They ate and slept underground and if they got "the call" they'd launch their missile, which was connected to other missiles, instigating nuclear warfare.

Wham bam blammo.

Here I was in the heart of one of our killing giants. All around me, nukes on high-alert status could be detonated at a moment's notice, wiping out millions.

We moved on through another long dark corridor where more of Gabriel's supplies lined the walls. He dropped his bag and gestured for me to do the same.

Then we approached the entryway to where the missile itself was once contained. Gabriel turned back as if to make sure I was still there. I followed him inside, bracing myself for a survivalist's cave, taking quick breaths in the cold air.

I couldn't see anything. Outside the flashlight's ray, the dark was so complete it was as if we were floating in utter blackness.

"I need to touch you," he said.

"My cell tracker's on."

He sighed. "I just mean … it's easier if I guide you."

He put a hand on my elbow and led me to the middle of the space.

"Wait here," he told me. The pitch-black silence was dizzying. I stumbled, trying to keep my balance.

There was a loud click then, like the sound of Hawthorn's football-stadium lights going on. My eyes were drawn to the spot of brightness where Gabriel stood by a big rectangular light on a tripod. He'd set these up in a circle around the circumference of the space and he began switching them on, one by one.

My gasp echoed back at me as I followed the light washing over the dome.

What I saw wasn't a big black hole or a bunker of doomsday supplies. Instead, what came into view were scenes of gold, silver and bronze carpeting the massive walls.

Images of palm trees, flowers and rivers. People dancing and feasting. There was a palace with gardens. Houses and a market and figures in long robes. Fantasy creatures, kids playing and old men kneeling to pray.

"What is this?" I murmured.

"A place a friend told me about," he said.

The dome was at least a hundred and fifty feet high, way bigger than the silos housing the Minutemen missiles. Minutemen were long and thin, emerging from Montana's soil like candles on a cake. This space looked to be ten times the diameter.

There was also a series of interconnected ladders zigzagging from the ground to the top, and scaffolding on wheels.

As if reading my mind, Gabriel explained, "It wasn't a Minuteman they had in here. There were more powerful nukes under development. They never got finished. They were called Typhons."

"It's … beautiful." My words were inadequate and I knew it.

"Still needs work." He looked up and pointed to the blast ceiling that I'd sat on outside. "When it's finished I want to blow that open. Get the light streaming in."

I approached to touch the walls, which had a 3-D feel to them, as if the images were about to float away. It was only when I looked closer that I realized what the scenes were made from.

Every single flower, plant, animal, person and pattern was composed of ammunition. There must have been tens of thousands of cartridges and casings on the walls, some shining like precious metals and some black, darkened by a blowtorch. And all around on the ground were pyramids of ammo. Cartridges thin as cigarettes, thick as lipsticks, dozens of different shapes and sizes in a tangle of copper, lead, brass and steel.

"I buy in bulk online," he explained. "And casings are common around here. I take walks or go to the ranges. Some's from Angstrom or Stelan. Taken illegally, I guess, but I figure I've put in my time." He paused. "I also brought some brass back."

"What? You're saying you fired, then …"

"I took from ground refuse. Security's loose coming home."

"Have your parents seen this?"

"I told 'em I was working on a thing. Dad's beyond caring. Mom never set foot in here. Says it's bad luck."

"Has anyone seen it?"

"Just you," he said. "And I'd appreciate you not telling your sidekick. I'm only showing you because I can't finish solo. I'm short on time."

It seemed to me he had plenty of time.

"You going on a trip or something?" I asked.

He dragged a cardboard box over to one of the pyramids and poured the casings onto the mound.

"I can pay you, but not much," he said.

I took in the mural again, confused that something so otherworldly could be made by a person whose life was ruled by combat and violence.

"Why are you doing this?" I asked.

He shrugged. "Just burning daylight."

I didn't know anything about him, really. Except that he was a former Marine who was making something unbelievable. And I wanted to be part of it.

"You don't have to pay me," I told him. "It's not like I have anything better to do."

And just like that I became Gabriel Finch's accomplice.

The missile dome was like the Shady Springs planetarium but with no stars or planets. It was dead quiet inside. You couldn't hear the wind or the birds, or any sign of life aside from our own breathing, which was magnified as we stood there not speaking.

I felt safe, as if nothing could get to me in there. As if the world outside no longer existed at all.

11

Half our town went to church and half were lapsed Christians. The Lees came from the lapsed side. We weren't believers but after seeing inside the silo, I felt like I'd witnessed a kind of miracle.

I couldn't wait to go back to the farm. I went to class and I played around with my camera. I made it through two shifts at Taco John's, and I even read *Supervolcano Mayhem!* which Nan bought me for the winter excursion to Yellowstone.

I couldn't make the next trip without Billy, either, who was over his flu. Before class we met at Hill 5 to watch the sunrise. The chinook was losing strength and the air was hazy. Indian summer turned the trees that had survived the early frost into torches, and hunters were out in the wooded valleys again.

Billy was late as usual. I sat on my backpack and watched the sun come up alone, slicing the town like a blade. As Angstrom's reveille bugle sounded, I called Mom.

"Everything okay?" There was less energy in her voice than the last time we'd spoken.

"Remember the Finch family?" I asked.

"Course I do. Sad, what happened to their girl."

"I'm doing my service hours on their farm. Helping the son."

"The one who went to the wars? Nancy always said that boy would go far."

"He didn't."

"Geographically speaking, he did."

"How's the hotel job, Mom?"

"I quit. To devote proper time to my painting. I'm going to try to sleep now. Night, Twinkles."

As she hung up I could see Billy approaching. He drove over the curb and onto the grass, hopped out of his Jeep and ran up the path.

"How much did you miss me?" he hollered as he threw his arms around me in a full body tackle.

I hadn't missed him as much as I thought I would. Until he kissed me.

"Like crazy," I said and added casually, "I had to go to the farm, by the way. Lucinda asked me to check in."

"Army Strong didn't give you a hard time?"

"He's okay."

"Alrighty then," he said, looking away.

I didn't bring up the silo. I'd never kept anything from Billy and I felt guilty. It wasn't my secret to tell, though.

I waited for him to ask more questions but he just looked out at Angstrom and its inhabitants, circulating the grid like ants. Then he flashed his dazzling smile and it was me who tackled him, and we got to class a half hour late.

After school we met up in the parking lot. Billy wanted to take the Jeep so I got my things out of the truck. Even before climbing in I noticed his cap. He never wore hats because it took him a long time to perfect his slightly messy hair each morning.

The cap was a collector's item. They sold them out of a locked display case at the Exxon on Main. The Operation Iraqi Freedom logo was on its badge: an eagle on top of the Middle East, and Baghdad clasped in its open beak like a jewel.

"Give it up," I said.

"What?"

"Quit trying to be ironic. You can't wear that."

"Why not?"

"You don't have the right."

"Cause I'm not a murderer?"

"We don't know what he did there. Maybe he built schools and gave out food. Or trained local soldiers to fight terrorists. Maybe he saved lives."

"Yeah. His own."

"Since when did you get so judgmental?"

"Since when did you get so into this guy?"

"I'm not. It's just that …"

"I don't come from Halo, so I don't get it. I'm aware of that. You hold it against me daily."

It was our first argument and I didn't even know what we were fighting about. We drove to the farm in silence until Billy parked near the barn and took the keys out of the ignition and we both just sat there.

"What's changed?" he finally said, giving me a hurt look.

"What do you mean?"

"You're acting different."

"No, I'm not."

Out in the field I could see Gabriel running with a big pack on his back, Storm keeping stride.

"Oorah!" Billy raised a fist in the air.

"Take it off," I pleaded.

Billy removed the ball cap and whipped it onto the backseat.

"I can't wait to get away from this rathole," he said, reaching for my hand. "You better not want to move back one day, like in the movies."

"Nah." I looked out at the vast tracts of nothing.

Billy puffed his cheeks and blew a blast of air out. "You know I'd do anything for you, right?"

"Ditto," I told him, softening. We kissed then, and it blurred my thinking. "Listen, Billy. He's got a project in the silo."

"You went *in* there?"

"Briefly."

"Jeez, Twy."

"My tracker was on."

Billy glared out the window at Gabriel, still running in the field.

"Let me guess. Fallout shelter."

"Nothing like that. It's actually really insane. It's this …" I couldn't come up with the words. "Remember Hooper's Sistine Chapel slideshow? That amazing ceiling painting?"

"You're comparing him to Michelangelo?"

"I just mean that's what it reminds me of. You have to see it. Only I'm not supposed to tell you."

"Charlie Foxtrot's got you keeping secrets from me?"

"Trust me. It's incredible."

"Trust you?"

"Did you notice …"

"What? Did I notice what, Twy?"

"Did you notice that he limps sometimes?"

Billy's face fell. He jumped out of the Jeep and slammed the door, while I looked out at Gabriel running like he had an enemy at his heels.

I caught up to Billy and we approached Gabriel near the bullet tree where he'd stopped to tie Storm when he saw us coming.

He took off his pack. Even though the air was cool, he was sweating.

I figured it was best to just come out with it.

"Billy knows," I told him. "I thought you could use the help."

Gabriel caught his breath. He took gulps from his canteen and looked at the sky, shaking his head.

"He won't tell anyone," I assured him.

"Yes, he will."

"Thanks for the vote of confidence," Billy said.

Gabriel was already walking toward the blast door.

"I couldn't care less about whatever it is you're doing," Billy called after him as we started for the silo. "I just want Twyla to get her hours."

I felt more confident passing through the cold, dank tunnel. Billy held my hand in the dark but he didn't say a word. When we entered the dome and Gabriel turned the lights on, Billy looked around, his mouth open.

"Seeing an actual missile would've been cooler," he said. "But this is interesting."

I pulled him aside. "We're going to help him finish it."

"Can't his commando pals do that?"

Gabriel stood near a pile of brass that went up to his knees. He pointed up a ladder to what appeared to be a gold-brown marshland. Above it was a half-completed flock of soaring birds with long broad wings.

"I'm working on the ibises. I need about seven hundred of these." He pulled a casing from the pile, pale gray like a winter moon. "They're rare. You'll need to sort through to find them."

I looked around at various outlines in black paint that hadn't yet been filled. Each area contained letters.

Gabriel pointed again. "For every section I've marked CAR for cartridge or CAS for casing, followed by color: BL for the torched blacks, S is silver, G for gray and a scale of 1 to 10 for shade, and GOL means Gold also scaled 1 to 10."

His system was no different from the paint-by-number kits Mom used to buy me at Dollar Tree.

"OCD much?" Billy asked. "Where'd you get all this junk?"

Gabriel approached him. "If you're not up for this, move out."

"It's all good," Billy said, glancing at me before extracting a casing from the pile. "How many of these bad boys, did you say?"

I tried to get comfortable on the cold ground and started sorting through a pyramid of ammo. Billy sat beside me and Gabriel climbed a ladder toward his birds. The three of us worked without talking for a while.

"Ever play tunes in here?" Billy called up to Gabriel. He was already losing interest.

"Uh-uh," Gabriel replied without looked down. He'd clipped a pouch around his waist and drew from it every few minutes.

"Acoustics would be dope." Billy gave a battle cry.

I snuck glances at Gabriel when I could. He went into a trancelike concentration while he worked. He had a precise system. Painting an outline, identifying each section with letters representing the ammo type and tone, then selecting corresponding supplies. He coated the concrete with adhesive before he pressed the ammo onto it, extracting each bit of metal from his pouch and polishing it with a cloth first. Then he held the ammo down on the wall until it was stuck in place.

The cartridges and casings were as tightknit as kernels on a cob. It was a meticulous process. Up on the scaffolding, as he tidied and arranged his stockpiles, he worked with a steady hand. The shakes I'd put down to PTSD were gone. It was as though he entered into a state of total relaxation.

Dipping into the cold pile of brass, my fingers stiffened, and I made a mental note to bring gloves next time.

Billy's phone alarm sounded. Our two hours were up. We'd never get anywhere in such short stints, and I wanted to stay. But I knew it would mean another fight.

I decided then to drop by to help Gabriel whenever I could, on my own.

It was a shock stepping outdoors again after being submerged in the silo's deep darkness. The sky seemed bluer than ever.

Gabriel trailed out after us, squinting at the sun. Billy put his hand up in a high five.

"Semper fi, man."

"See you around," Gabriel said, without high-fiving him back.

"You've got to stop trying so hard," I told Billy as we walked to the Jeep.

As we pulled away, Gabriel untied Storm from the bullet tree. He picked up a piece of rope and played tug of war with the dog and they rolled around in the dirt. I even thought I heard Gabriel laugh.

But it could just have been the wind blowing through the barn's loose planks.

12

"What was Gabriel Finch good at when you taught at Hawthorn?" I asked Nan. I was helping her install a seat heater. We were on our knees in the Airstream, with wrenches and screwdrivers from Grandpa Wallace's old toolbox.

"He was a poetry buff," she said, testing out her seat. "Straight As in my class. Up until Elsie, that is."

"Was he nice?"

"Don't recall otherwise. He was courteous and amiable to us teachers."

"What about girlfriends?"

Nan sized me up. "Footballers always had girls hanging off them. Same then as now."

"So he probably had a girlfriend."

"He probably had many. But after his sister's death he was a loner. That, I remember." She put the drill down and reached for a wrench. "You've taken a keen interest in your volunteering, Twinks. He's got you doing farm chores, has he?"

"Yeah. Hey, Nan."

"Mhmm."

"What are those mural things called again, in art?"

"Mural things?"

"You know, when the walls are covered with pictures and patterns made of rocks and glass and stuff."

"Mosaics?"

"Exactly. Mosaics."

She went back to tightening the seat. She wore a white crochet-like shirt but when you got up close you saw skulls. Gabriel's mosaic was like Nan's skull top. Pretty and delicate from far away, until you got near and saw what was really there.

I rubbed the fabric between my fingers.

"Did you know there are skulls all over your top?" I asked, fiddling with my camera to take a photo.

Nan crinkled her nose, looking down at the shirt.

"I had no idea. Got it at the Sally Ann. My eyes are going."

I snapped a few shots and stood to leave.

"Be careful with that boy," Nan said. "You may think you'll grow to understand his trauma, but you won't."

"I'm just doing my service hours," I said. "What's there to be careful about anyway?"

"Your heart, granddaughter." She raised a knuckly hand to her chest and pressed it against the skulls.

Later on, I headed to the farm while Billy was at Affinity working on business-school applications. Martin Goodwin said he'd back the catering company in California if Billy also did business school on a part-time basis. I didn't see the point in telling him about my unscheduled drop-ins.

By the time I pulled up, the sky was a deepening blue. When Gabriel opened the screen door, Storm pounced on me. I pushed the slobbering dog away as Gabriel wiped his hands with the cloth he always had sticking out of his back pocket. I got a stick and tossed it as far off the porch as I could, and the dog went running after it.

Gabriel rolled a red wagon from the barn over to the house and piled it high with boxes of ammo. I wondered if it had been Elsie's.

As we walked to the launch pad, a grasshopper landed on his chest. With his free hand he picked it off and swallowed it. Another landed on his arm, and he offered it to me.

"I ate already, thanks," I told him.

"Some day you may need the protein."

"Wouldn't it be nice if we could not obsess over End Times so much around here?" I said.

"Not going to happen." He turned to yank the wagon from a divot.

"My dad thinks Yellowstone's going to erupt," I said as we kept walking.

"Could be."

In the late afternoon light, I could see faint lines on his forehead and crow's-feet extending from his eyes, even though he was only a few years older than me.

He caught me watching him. "I'm still pissed that you told him. In case you're wondering."

He pulled open the enormous door and I followed him into the darkness.

Inside the dome, he dumped box after box of ammo on an old parachute cloth. I went back and forth between the piles, organizing, until I noticed that he was the one watching me now.

"Is there a problem?" I asked.

"There's no problem." He limped as he walked over.

"What's with the limp?"

"Arthritis," he said. "From combat. And playing ball, probably. It's in my fingers, too." He looked down at his hands. "Flares up sometimes."

Suddenly his face looked battered.

"What's your real aim with the mural?" I asked. "Just tell me straight up."

"So I don't frag out."

"Frag out?"

"Take a frag, pull the pin and drop it under my shirt."

Gabriel threw his hammer down and sat against the wall. I sat beside him. When he pulled his knees up to his chest, I noticed how thin and worn his socks were. He put his head in his hands, massaging his temples.

"We went on a crisis-response mission near a place called Uruk this one time," he said. "About 150 miles from Baghdad. Ever heard of it?"

I shook my head and rubbed at my boots.

"Uruk's the oldest city in the world. The first, biggest, longest-lived Mesopotamian city."

"Meso what?"

"Mesopotamia. The ancient region that included a chunk of Iraq. I mean, these were the first people to grow wheat. And to divide time up like we use it now. It's where the first organized governments happened. And the first form of writing was found there, on clay tablets."

I felt like a country bumpkin. "Is the mosaic Uruk?" I asked.

He nodded. "The place is way older than the Bible. Or Christianity, or Islam. And we passed by on mission like it was no biggie. Our interpreter wouldn't shut up about the site. And I took a leak and got back into the Humvee as fast as I could and we moved on."

He reached into the plastic bag beside him and cracked open a beer. "The city was surrounded by a wall built by Gilgamesh, the king. Only part of it's been dug up."

"Why were you there again?"

He ignored my question. "Some of the first mosaics ever made were in Uruk. Mosaics that lasted through thousands of years of war. I was standing in the cradle of civilization. In full battle rattle. And I didn't give a fuck." When he turned to me with those eyes of his, I had to look down as he went on. "After I got home all I could think about was that place. The five minutes we spent there in the scorching heat. The deafening quiet of that sanctuary where we were trespassing."

He slammed back his beer in one gulp. His fist came down on the empty like a mallet, forming a flat silver circle like a medal.

"I need more cartridges, Twyla."

I got up and went over to the nearest box of ammo. "Gold okay?"

"More than what you've got there."

He picked up a flashlight, put his hand on it and started turning it on and off.

"Family's broke. There were too many bills when Elsie was sick. My parents can't keep up the mortgage payments for much longer. Not that it matters."

It was the first time he'd mentioned his sister.

I looked around the dome.

"But … what will happen to this?" I asked.

Gabriel approached a wall and put a hand on a palm tree. "I'm guessing the Forces'll implode it. And so be it. So long as I finish."

I walked the circumference of the mosaic. Confiscating it would be a crime. People had to see it.

Art had been one of my junior-year electives. I was terrible at painting and drawing, but I'd learned about perspective, movement, harmony and unity. Even I knew that what Gabriel was making was extraordinary.

I kept looking around, touching the kaleidoscope of metals, thinking.

"I've got a way for you to make money," I finally told him.

He gave a few slow blinks. "Don't keep me in suspense."

"There's this big art contest in New York. Anyone can enter."

He went back to his polishing.

"The prize is a hundred grand."

"It'd be a waste of time."

"I'll take the pictures. I'll fill out the application."

"How's that going to help me now?"

"Your mom said she'd transfer funds into my account for food and utilities soon. Seeing as you've got your tasty MREs, you can use the food portion for ammo." I followed him as he walked off. "You could save the farm with the winnings."

He climbed the scaffolding.

"So I'll go ahead and enter you?" I called up.

"You're a pain in the backend," he told me, glancing down.

I waited.

"Knock yourself out," he finally said.

13

The days got shorter, with more darkness stretching out at each end. Dusk then night spread above town, thick as an oil slick.

Dad came home again. He spent his time in the mini casinos scattered along the highway, gathering there with his friends like these places were wishing wells. He made me drop him off and pick him up at a different one each afternoon.

I didn't tell Nan. The Yellowstone money was due soon and he still hadn't paid up.

One day after class I found Nan in a foldout lounger on the driveway, catching the afternoon's last rays. She'd propped the recliner against the Airstream where the sun was warmest. Behind her, the silver vehicle gleamed and let off heat.

She was working on another poem. Dried brown leaves rattled around us.

"What's today's theme?" I asked.

"Hay fever," she told me, sneezing. She lifted her sunglasses to look at me. "Your father's in a mood. Probably best to ignore him."

I went inside and found Dad at the kitchen table, empties lined up in front of him like bowling pins. The TV was on. Jake and Julia Pritchett appeared in a commercial, holding balloons and leaning against a charcoal SUV at their dad's dealership.

I took a plastic bag from a drawer, emptied the dregs into the sink and threw the cans into it.

"She wore this cream on her face at night," Dad said.

"Huh?"

"Your mother. Wore this invisible cream that tasted awful. I couldn't kiss her."

"I doubt it was on purpose." I put a hand on his shoulder.

He stood and turned off the TV.

"I need a lift to Reg's," he told me. Which meant a bender before leaving for the patch.

"Do you have the money for my field trip?" I asked.

"Not yet. Don't worry about it."

His fingers were yellow and dirty. He needed a shave and a shower. When I'd asked Nan why she didn't put her foot down all she said was, "One day he'll get tired of dwelling on regret. Hold tight."

Before bed I read up on America's Next Great Artist.

MoMA is searching the country for America's best up-and-coming artist, the homepage read. *Tell us what you think of the contenders as they progress through the competition toward the prize of $100,000 and exhibiting at MoMA in New York. Stay tuned in February to vote for your favorite work of art!*

Following online public voting to determine the top ten works, appointed judges picked the three finalists, then the winner. The judging panel consisted of one of MoMA's chief curators, Elizabeth Malone, an internationally renowned artist called Renny, and an art critic named Zohar Berkowitz.

The finalists would be flown to New York for a gala ceremony. Third place received five grand, second received ten, and first place won a hundred grand. Besides the cash prize, it was considered a career launcher for artists, since the museum put the winner's work up in their galleries, which saw millions of visitors yearly.

I studied the rules closely. The deadline for submissions was January 15th, just over two months away.

Veterans Day came. We got the day off school. Angstrom and Fort Stelan orchestrated a big parade that wove through Halo like a boa constrictor. Tanks formed a circle in the town square, their gun turrets aimed at the crowds in starburst formation.

There was a ceremony and WWII aircraft and parachuters. Flags everywhere. Early-bird specials and bargain shopping, and current and former military members with valid ID ate free at Applebee's and Chili's. Taco John's paid us time and a half and we offered free fajitas to vets.

When I got to work, Jolene was sitting on the counter talking to Travis. Across the food court Carmen Lopez watched us.

"Mexicans go mental for weddings and babies. You'd better pop the question soon, Trav. What is she, like, twenty?" Jolene stared at Carmen. "I'm famished, guys. Could I get some potato olés?"

I stuck a fork into a container of fried nuggets and handed it to Jolene. Then I went to the workstation to pre-layer tacos.

"Got a nutritional chart?" Jolene called out as she stuffed her mouth.

Carmen came over then, hands on her hips.

"This isn't real Mexican," she told Travis, ignoring Jolene. When she spoke you could see her tongue ring, a little silver barbell. Her black hair was coiled into a tight bun at the nape of her neck. "Lemme cook for you."

"Gosh, Carm. I'd like that," Travis said.

She walked off, rear end swaying back and forth in her brown polyblend uniform.

"Booty call," Jolene said.

Then Jeremy showed up with his dad's ID card. Apparently Jolene had texted him.

I pulled her aside as Travis served him. "Why are you hanging with that jerkoff?"

"Jer-bear's not so bad." She pushed her olés away.

Jeremy came over with a fast-food bag under each arm.

"You tell Twat about her war hero?"

"Get lost, Jeremy." I turned my back to him.

"My old man says Finchy was involved in a major clusterfuck."

"What's he talking about?" I asked Jolene.

"Stupid rumors, Twizzles."

Jeremy caused trouble and picked fights wherever he went. He was a loose cannon and a liar. But his comment bugged me.

"As if Hooper would send us, nice try," I called out as they walked off together.

I didn't think Gabriel would be at the farm when I went there after work. I figured he'd be occupied with ceremonies all day. I'd only stopped by to Skype Lucinda, so she'd see that I was there.

But when I let myself in, I found him on the living-room floor, leaning against the couch, surrounded by books.

"What are you doing here?" I asked.

"I live here."

"Don't you have Veterans Day stuff to go to?"

"I don't participate."

I noticed the half-empty bottle of Jim Beam next to some beers.

"Shouldn't you be working on your mural?" I sat down cross-legged beside him. He balanced a large book on his knees, open to a page with a marble mask on it. "What's that?" I asked.

"The Lady of Uruk," he said. "One of the earliest makings of the human face." He touched the image. "Looted from the National Museum during the Fall of Baghdad. Babylonian, Sumerian, Assyrian collections. Rare Islamic texts. All gone. Our troops did jack."

"It's not like you were there," I told him. "You went ages later."

"Things are worse now. These countries' histories are being obliterated by militants with sledgehammers and bulldozers, or by drone strikes, accidentally by us, or whatever." He took a swig and turned the page to a hunting scene of warriors on horseback chasing gazelles, just as Storm came in with the shower scrub brush in his mouth.

The dog dropped the brush at my feet.

Gabriel set the book aside and put his hand on Storm's muzzle.

"They were going to put him down," he said, looking into the dog's dark eyes. "He wasn't obeying orders anymore. So I took him."

I picked up the scrub brush as Gabriel ran a hand through his hair. When he stretched and yawned, his T-shirt lifted and I saw his abdomen. I turned the brush around in my hands. What I held had washed his body countless times. I tossed it across the room for Storm.

Gabriel crushed a few empties with a closed fist. Then he tilted his head back on the couch and put his hand on my boot like he didn't even know he was doing it. I watched his hand resting there. Felt it through the leather.

"I'm so damn tired," he said, closing his eyes.

Veterans Day explosions detonated in the distance but Gabriel didn't react. I tapped his shoulder. He opened his eyes and looked at me.

"Are you okay?" I asked. He studied my lips as I spoke.

"Ringing's bad today." He pointed to his ear.

"Almost forgot. Your mom deposited the money," I said to cheer him up.

"Great," he said, forcing a smile.

I picked up the book of poems that lay at his feet.

When I flipped through it, grains of sand fell from the pages.

14

Dad went back to the rigs. Even though I knew I wouldn't find anything, I scoured the house for the Yellowstone money. When I texted him about it he didn't respond.

It was too cold to sit outside anymore. I picked Billy up for class and we parked on Hill 5, staying in the truck with our coffees.

Dolly Parton and Kenny Rogers sang "Islands in the Stream" on the radio, until Billy turned off the music.

"How come you're so quiet these days?" he asked.

"Just drained, I guess." I put my head on his shoulder as I scrolled through my phone.

I looked at the America's Next Great Artist site until Billy took the phone from me and skimmed the rules, which I'd already memorized. When I'd told him about my plans to enter the mosaic in the contest, he'd rolled his eyes.

He handed my phone back. "He won't win."

"You don't know that."

"He's not right in the head, Twy. How many hours left?"

"I don't know. You don't have to come."

"Yeah, I do. Anyway, you need to get motivated."

"Get motivated?"

"Do something with yourself. Start focusing on our company."

"You mean your dad's company."

"Only till we buy him out."

"I'm graduating. Doesn't that count? And unlike some of us, I have a job."

"Those aren't achievements."

"I consider getting out of bed every day a major achievement," I told him. "And what about the mosaic?"

"Gluing garbage to walls isn't an achievement either."

"It's called contemporary art, Billy."

"A waste of time's what it is."

"I've been thinking I'll take pictures. Like, be a photographer. Someday."

"You said you'd shoot my dishes. But you never do."

"I haven't gotten around to it."

"You're always shooting anything and everything else."

"I'm trying to find my inspiration. These things take time."

"So you don't think my food's inspiring."

"Of course I do. But I might want to shoot other stuff, too." I thought about the wood grain elevators towering over our prairies like upright coffins while they slowly decomposed. And the silos dotting our pastures, the flat slabs of concrete standing out like crop circles in the fields. "Maybe landscapes. Or people."

Billy shook his head like he was disappointed in me.

"You can't make a living off that," he said. "Just like you can't make a living off pictures of Dumpsville, USA. Nobody wants to see those. Food and fashion. That's where the money's at."

I knew I needed to start figuring out my future, aside from the catering company. Billy would study and surf. I needed something that was mine. But I didn't feel like locking it in on the spot like Billy wanted.

And the more I thought about it, the more I wanted to put my own plans on hold until the contest deadline. Gabriel's mosaic was mind-blowing. I wanted him to win the prize money not only to save the farm, but also because he deserved to be recognized as an artist.

It started to snow. From Hill 5 I looked out at Halo's town hall. I took a few pictures, blurring the flakes on the windshield to focus on the gargoyles that jutted from the building's clock tower like fists.

"You haven't talked about California lately," Billy said.

The truth was, I hadn't thought about California in weeks.

"The SAT's distracting me," I explained. "And Nan wants to have a big Christmas lunch. She's invited my mom, if you can believe it. I know she won't come. But the way my dad's acting these days, it's going to be an epic fail regardless."

"That's what's stressing you out?" He sounded relieved.

I nodded but couldn't look him in the eye, so I stared down at my camera.

"Can you bring dessert?" I added.

"We're going to Chicago to see my grandparents."

"For how long?" I asked, discouraged.

"All of break."

"At least we have Yellowstone to look forward to," I told him.

"And California," he added, removing the elastic from my braid. "C'mere Pocahontas." He pulled me closer and we watched the snow fall.

Later, we took speakers into the silo. When we got to the farm, Billy wouldn't get out of the truck until I tied Storm to the plow. Nobody was in the house so we trekked through the white field, Billy sliding and slipping in his suede loafers. He refused to wear boots, a habit that I used to find quirky but more recently found annoying.

The blast door was wide open. Gabriel was expecting us.

Inside the missile dome we found him up on the scaffolding, his headlamp illuminating a new scene of animals including a tiger, a bear and a lion, in a spot that had been nothing but concrete the last time we were there.

"Noah's freakin' ark in here," Billy muttered before shuffling off to set the speakers up by a light stand.

I waved at Gabriel. He climbed down a ladder, then jumped and landed in front of me.

"Hi," I said, straightening as we stood facing each other in the half-light. I pointed to the new panel. "That's really something."

"Most of these animals died."

"Oh."

"Zoo workers had to stop feeding them before the first invasion. They were stolen for food or they starved in their cages. The ones found roaming around were shot. There was this really old Siberian tiger. And a blind brown bear."

Billy fiddled with the speakers, trying to turn the sound down. "Wildwood Flower" by the Carter Family came on.

The song carried through the space and reverberated around us.

I'd grown up listening to Dad strumming it. The slow picking and Mother Maybelle's scratch-style playing and the harmonizing voices made this simple melody one of the prettiest I knew.

I hummed along.

Oh, he taught me to love him and called me his flow'r / that was blooming to cheer him through life's dreary hour ...

Gabriel looked my way. My eyes followed the scar on his face, shaped like a question mark.

"You know this tune doesn't end well," he said. When he

smiled, dimples formed beneath his stubble.

"Yeehaw!" Billy hollered. Then he switched the music to Linkin Park and started rapping.

Gabriel walked over to the speakers and turned them off without so much as looking at Billy. Then he briefed us on our tasks. From the piles of cartridges and casings, we were to locate five shades of gold for the animals.

"Cool fact, did you know that Enola is alone spelled backwards?" Billy asked him.

"Aren't you going to set your timer?" Gabriel asked.

"No, man. We can stay as long as you need us."

Gabriel raised an eyebrow.

I'd thrown extra clothes into my pack and put on my toque and fleece. I even had a blanket for the ground. I spread it out and began sorting through the ammo.

Across the dome, Gabriel put his gas mask on and picked up the blowtorch. When he aimed his flame at the wall to darken it, the metals took on the shape of a pathway winding through dunes.

While he was polishing a section with his cloth, Billy called out, "Can you direct me to the facilities, cap'n?"

"Use the house," Gabriel told him. "Plumbing's no good in here."

When Billy left I went over to another new panel that wasn't there before, lower to the ground. It depicted a young couple crouched against the palace wall, holding hands and looking intently at one another. Between the rows of cartridges and casings were strands of colored beads.

"Who are they?" I asked.

"Our interpreter, Ali. And his fiancée, Nasreen." Gabriel came over and touched the beads. "Misbaha," he said. "Prayer beads. Locals sold these to us as souvenirs."

I took a few steps back to better admire the picture, he like a prince and she like a veiled princess, the both of them with emerald eyes. Yet the way the figures knelt so closely together made it seem like they were hiding.

I realized then that Gabriel created scenes before the bad stuff happened. Before the bombs dropped and the people and the animals died. The moments before everything turned.

In his art there were set boundaries and order. A kind of symmetry. Those rules that went out the window during a war.

My fingers ached from the repetitive movements of sorting through the ammo and I rubbed them.

Gabriel reached his hand out. "May I?" he asked.

He removed my fingerless gloves and pressed on my palms with his thumbs. Then he drew them along my lifelines. The pressure points he was getting to unsteadied me.

"Should've warned you. There's no way around the cramping," he said.

Only when I heard Billy barreling down the ramp did I pull my hands away from his.

Afterwards, while they both worked, I took pictures of the entire mosaic for the contest, including the wall of animals and the crouching lovers, the most spectacular sections so far.

We finished for the day and returned outdoors. Gabriel looked at the sky and breathed in the cold air, while Billy walked ahead of us to take a call from his dad.

As we made our way back to the farmhouse, Gabriel rolled up his sleeves, and I could see the black script on his forearm running from his elbow to his wrist like the imprints of bird feet.

"What's it say?" I asked.

He rubbed his arm and glanced at it. "Lines from the *Epic of Gilgamesh*."

96

"King of Uruk?"

He nodded. "Good memory."

"I've never seen lettering like that."

"It's cuneiform script."

"What's the epic about?"

"The adventures of King Gilgamesh. Oldest written story on earth."

"What kinds of adventures?" I persisted.

"That's for another time," he said.

15

On a night off from Taco John's I set up my makeshift darkroom in the bathroom. Nan had kept Grandpa Wallace's equipment for me, including a freezer full of film and printing paper. I also inherited his safelight, his developing tank, his enlarger and trays, and his sealed, premixed processing chemicals.

I liked the ritual of developing the way Grandpa Wallace had done it, the smell of the solutions and the orange-tinted lighting in the room. Most of all I loved watching an image slowly reveal itself beneath liquid in a tray, discovering what I hadn't noticed when I first snapped the shot.

I put a piece of plywood across the tub, where I placed three trays, and I added another board beside it for the enlarger. I turned off the light and loaded my film onto the developing reel, inserted the reel in its tank on the counter, closed the lid and developed, fixed and washed the film. I hung it to dry, speeding things up with a hairdryer. Then I turned on the safelight to enlarge and print the photos.

Setting the timer, I processed the prints, and Gabriel's image gradually materialized from when I'd shot him and Storm without him knowing. I examined his eyes, lips and nose, his jawline and his scar. Then I pulled a clothesline across my bedroom and hung the photos to dry. I lay on my bed and took in the mosaic, and Gabriel, floating above me.

Later I joined Nan in the kitchen, where she sat eating storebought apple turnovers, her favorite dessert.

"Did Grandpa ever photograph normal people?" I asked.

"Define normal."

"People around Halo. Ex-military. Or plant workers, or riggers."

"Shoot what moves you."

"That's not what I'm asking."

"Show me what you developed tonight."

"Plates of food."

"He preferred being in the hot spots." She wiped her hands. "Sometimes I thought your grandpa had a death wish."

"How come?"

"He was like those mechanical bull riders in bars. Think they won't get thrown off. They hold on awhile because their bodies are elasticky from drink. But it's always just a matter of time before they get tossed and break something." She brushed crumbs from her lap. "There's a waiver for riding those bulls so no one's liable. Same thing in the wars."

Over the weekend, when half of Halo was away at Pendletown's annual livestock fair and auction, Angstrom announced it was closing. The base would be relocating in six months.

Nobody was surprised. Angstrom's outdated buildings and equipment were no longer up to acceptable standards.

Mayor Tubman followed Angstrom's announcement with his own statement, assuring everyone that the base's closure wouldn't have a negative impact on Halo. New jobs would be created at Sunnyside. Like working at the hog plant was incentive enough for everyone to stick around.

But we all knew that without the base, our town would eventually be decommissioned.

I wondered if Angstrom would leave their Triple Ds behind, or if they'd take them along like ailing relatives. Of course, only the base would move. The ICBMs would stay in our great plains forever, or until they were launched.

It was possible that the Air Force was planning some big attack. The wars were heating up again. A lot of our jets had stopped flying over football games to go and drop bombs in the Middle East.

Maybe Angstrom wanted to save the citizens of Halo in case of retaliation, and this was their way of evacuating us, the aging infrastructure just an excuse. But I doubted it. Like the casualties in those faraway countries, we'd be counted as collateral damage.

What unsettled me more than Angstrom was the news that Mom was coming home for Christmas. She wanted to see me, she said, and she had some loose ends to tie up with Dad. She'd made arrangements to stay with Jackie and Jolene Bolton.

In class Jolene went on about it, chewing on her pen, crossing and uncrossing her legs in the aisle. She wore a kilt and knee-high boots, her lips coated in a shiny lacquer.

"You should stay over when your mom's here. We'll drink coolers and sneak out," she told me.

Hooper finally got around to collecting Yellowstone fees. At the same time, she noted where we were at with our community service hours. She gave me an inquisitive look as she took my money and checked my name off. Dad hadn't come through. I'd used a chunk of my California savings instead.

"How is the aid work going with Lucinda Finch's boy?" she asked.

"Fine."

"Hours to date?"

"Twenty," I lied. I didn't bother keeping track of my time anymore. I'd gone beyond the forty-hour mark but I didn't want Hooper wondering why I was still going.

"And what exactly are you doing there?"

"Cleaning. Sorting through stuff."

"Billy says the three of you are fast friends now. Have the Help a Vet folks checked in?"

"Mhmm."

To boot, we had to dissect fetal pigs in bio lab. Our teacher, Hank Dodge, got them over at Sunnyside Farms. Jolene and Crystal followed along on computers set up against the back wall, which had software that took them through the dissecting process.

"It's animal cruelty," Jolene said theatrically. Although she worked at Sunnyside, she never went into the plant.

"They're dead, Jolene," Dodge said. "Use the computer and don't disrupt us."

Billy and I paired up. In our white lab coats and goggles we looked ready to invent the next atomic bomb. Inside its tray, the pig was sucked of its juices and wrinkly.

Inhaling the antiseptic smell of formaldehyde, Billy put the knife down straight after picking it up.

"I don't know what's wrong with me," he said. "Weak stomach, I guess."

I took over. "I got it," I told him.

He grabbed my hand then. "Let's get engaged," he whispered.

I laughed until I looked at his tense face. "We haven't even lived together."

"We know we love each other so why not?" His words came out rushed, panicked.

I wrapped his arms around my waist. "You don't have to worry," I told him.

"Worry about what?"

"The Marine."

Billy stepped back and took off his lab coat.

"It's just … you act immature around him sometimes," I said. "And I know that's not the real you."

He looked at me like he was genuinely thinking it over.

"You're right," he said. "Stupid idea."

He excused himself to go to the washroom.

I took deep breaths until I stopped feeling queasy. Billy had just proposed in a lab full of carcasses.

I picked up the scalpel to make the incision down the ventral side of the pig like Dodge had instructed. But as I tried to concentrate, something hit my neck and landed at my feet.

Jeremy and Troy sniggered from the work station behind me. On the ground beside my boot was this tiny organ that could only be a heart. I bent and scooped it up and placed it in the tray.

The animal's snout pointed at me, its tail curled like a fiddlehead fern. I closed my eyes, pretending it was Jeremy, and cut the body from its neck to its groin. The knife went through easily. The fetal pig had been injected with a colored rubber compound, and the arteries and veins filled with red and blue latex were somehow beautiful.

When Dodge wasn't looking I threw the heart back at Jeremy. It went flying past him and hit Jolene in the head instead, but she had so many hair extensions that she didn't notice. The heart was that light.

16

The next time we went into the silo, I saw a lot more cans on the ground. I wondered how much Gabriel drank. There was always an open beer at his side while he worked.

Billy made a production of crinkling the empties in his hand.

"Take the pain! Take it! Dance, you one-legged mother-fucker! Dance!" He stuck two cans in front of his eyes. "Ever seen *Platoon*?"

Gabriel checked his watch. "Time to do some banking."

He wanted to withdraw the funds that Lucinda had deposited into my account for his supplies.

"Let's jet," Billy told him. "Twyla can hang back."

"I have to go," I said. "The money's in my account."

"So we'll all go."

"There's room for two in the cab," Gabriel said.

Billy turned to me. "Then do an e-transfer. From here. With your phones."

"Need to make a pickup from the post office. I've gotta sign or they won't release it," Gabriel replied.

"We'll be quick," I told Billy.

He pulled me in and kissed me for an extra-long time before he sat back down on the blanket and launched a game on his phone.

We tied Storm up outside and Gabriel asked if I'd drive. He had a truck at the farm, but since he'd gotten a DUI, he was overly cautious not to lose his license again.

As we drove along the highway Gabriel looked out at the farmland. It was a clear day and the sun made the snow in the fields sparkle. I wondered if he was having flashbacks of the wars, staring at the powdery dunes.

It was Saturday and a lot of townies were out running errands or meeting at Michelle's, the local diner. On Main Street, friends of Nan's saw me and waved, then did a double take when they noticed their former football hero in the passenger seat.

"I guess you don't come into town much," I commented.

"You'll have to show me what I've been missing."

"Sweet fuck all," I told him.

Thanksgiving had come and gone. People were busy replacing gourds and rubber turkeys with elves and inflatable snowmen.

We walked two blocks down Main to the bank, past Shriners in club jackets hanging wreaths on the streetlamps, and shop owners stringing lights and decorations in their display windows.

I stopped in front of the post office but Gabriel didn't go in. When I called after him he said he forgot he'd already picked up his parcel.

Despite the pre-Christmas buzz, there were new ads on storefronts beside the usual *No Guns Allowed* signs. *Liquidation, 70% Off Everything, Everything Must Go.*

At this rate, Halo would shut down before Angstrom even moved.

In the bank I got a funny look from the teller, Mom's old friend Deb Higgins.

"Looks like you're doing a lot of holiday shopping this year," she said. I smiled as she counted the bills. "Or is this for college? You know, you can pay your deposit directly through us. We can transfer the funds for you."

I put my hand out and she had no choice but to give me the money.

"Have a nice day," I told her.

I placed the cash in an envelope and offered it to Gabriel, who was eating a donut by the bank's festive display, consisting of a train set on a table. Together we observed the little black caboose and passenger cars go around an oval track. The words *Western Spirit* were painted on the side of the caboose, and in the middle of the oval was a model of our town, surrounded by cotton. A version of "Have Yourself a Merry Little Christmas" made up of jingling bells played on a loop.

"Angstrom's missing," Gabriel said, watching the train go around.

He didn't want to do a straight-up transfer because he thought the teller would call his mother. So we walked a few more blocks down Main to the machines outside the Exxon. Gabriel deposited the full thousand onto his credit card so he could buy ammo online.

A truck drove by as we stood at the intersection where stores ended and the road continued out of town. I made out three hulky bodies in its cab, each of them in shades and a cap.

The driver's window came down.

"Finchyyyyyyyy!" he called out, then another head poked forward as the truck flew past. "Waddup, bitches!"

I assumed it was football players or some of Gabriel's battle buddies.

Gabriel raised a hand in a stiff wave. He watched the truck speed down the road. It was cold and I wanted to get going but he just stood there. I followed his gaze until I realized that it wasn't the truck he was looking at anymore. Directly before us, in the last block of storefronts, was Miss Irene's Studio.

"Elsie danced there," he told me. "I used to drive her. To lessons."

As I tried to come up with something to say, I heard screeching tires. The truck had turned around and was accelerating back toward us.

An arm reached out from the passenger window and threw something at Gabriel, hard and fast.

"Traitorrrr!" After the object hit Gabriel he ducked, hand to his head, a delayed reaction. A beer can smacked and burst against the sidewalk.

I couldn't chase after them fast enough to read the plate. They'd veered off onto a side street and were already gone.

I ran over to Gabriel. His temple was split open and his forehead was bleeding.

"I'm taking you to the hospital," I told him.

"Let's go home," he said.

"Did you know those thugs?"

"Nope. I'm fine."

He retrieved the foaming can from the snow and took swigs from it until it was empty, then tossed it in the direction the truck had gone.

I pulled Taco John's napkins from my coat pocket and reached up to his forehead.

When he objected I cut him off. "Keep pressing till we get to the farm, or we're going to Emergency."

As we walked back to the truck, someone stopped us.

"Everything all right?" a Shriner asked, coming down from his ladder.

"Yessir," Gabriel replied. "These decorations are splendiferous," he added, glancing up at the wreaths.

The Shriner grinned, revealing perfect false teeth. "Be sure not to miss the lights display at town hall."

"Wouldn't miss it for the world." Gabriel shook the old man's hand.

"Sonny!" the Shriner called out as we walked on. Gabriel and I both turned.

"You've done well, serving our country," he told him, making a small arm salute.

"Likewise," Gabriel said, but his voice had gone dull.

"How did he know?" I asked.

"Being in the military's like being in the mob. Once you're in you can't get out."

As we drove back to the farm, I glimpsed Gabriel in my peripheral vision. He sat very still. I handed him more napkins to stop the bleeding. Then he asked me to pull over so he could get snow for the cut. I parked by the river and we looked for some ice along the edge of the bank.

Guys beat on each other a lot in Halo. Our town was full of rednecks. But what had just happened to Gabriel in plain daylight on the street scared me. It wasn't drunks pounding on each other for fun. It was a targeted attack on a football hero and a vet of two tours. Now that he'd turned his back on the wars, maybe some locals considered him a traitor.

I tried not to think about Jeremy's hints that Gabriel had done something bad over there. Something worse than usual. I had to have faith that Gabriel would eventually tell me about whatever had happened.

Skaters were out already, even though the river had only recently hardened and the rink wasn't officially open. Teenagers, mostly. Daredevils who never considered that the water might not be frozen enough yet, and that death could snatch them up at any time.

From where we stood we could hear the rhythmic scraping of their skates. Gabriel held the chunk of ice to his forehead and I looked up at him every so often while he watched the figures slip and spin as they flew past us.

"Splendiferous?" I asked.

"When something's more than splendid. Like that smile of yours."

I felt lightheaded as I looked off at the skaters again.

Back at the farm we found Billy firing at the oak tree.

"*Boom*. Nailed it!" he yelled after each round.

He stopped when he saw Gabriel's cut. "What'd you do, hold up the bank?"

"I'm done for today," Gabriel said, heading toward the farmhouse.

"Told you he's a ticking time bomb." Billy came up beside me, put his arm around my shoulder and pulled me in. "What happened?"

"It was only a scuffle."

"Tell me what went down, Twyla."

"Nothing," I said. "He bumped into some friends. They messed around on the street."

We heard a blast, followed by several more blasts. Another drill over at Angstrom.

Billy went back to shooting. "Snap!" he cried.

"Do you have iodine? Band-Aids?" I called out to Gabriel.

"Got it all," he said and kept going, his head bent low and his hands shoved in his pockets.

As he walked away I took his picture. And then I took another one of his shadow in the snow, elongated and dark before him. And when he got too far away I used my infinity focus for one last shot.

17

Nan had begun planning her journey with paper maps, which she spread out on the kitchen table. First she'd drive north to British Columbia and Alberta. Then she'd head east, through Saskatchewan and Manitoba, Ontario and Quebec, all the way to the Gaspé Peninsula and Newfoundland and Labrador. She wanted to see the Pierced Rock, a huge formation in the Gulf of St. Lawrence with a hole in it.

"Charlie called," she told me. "She'll be here Saturday."

"Does Dad know?"

"I'll tell him tomorrow, unless you want to do the honors."

"No, thanks. When's he home?"

"Christmas Eve."

"Billy can't come."

"Dang. I was counting on his Johnnycake cobblers."

"I'll pick up an ice cream log."

"Good enough. And I've invited Jolene and Jackie. To deflect."

"Can Trav and Carm come, too? They've got no family here."

"The more the merrier."

My phone dinged. A text from Lucinda Finch. *Won't be home for Christmas. Let's chat.*

I'd convinced Gabriel to tell his mom about the contest. Since then, she'd been checking in more often.

Nan peered over my shoulder.

"Lame," I said. "The Finches aren't coming for the holidays."

"Bring him," she replied.

"Here?"

"Yes, Twyla. Invite Gabriel Finch to our home for Christmas luncheon."

I went to my room and phoned him. As usual he didn't pick up so I left a message.

"Hey. Nan wants you to come for Christmas. I mean, I do, too. Let me know." I hung up then called back right away. "It's Twyla," I said and hung up again.

Within minutes he texted.

Do you have a tree?

No

Want one?

Sure

I'll need a ride

Done

Billy aced the SAT and term exams, and I got by with average scores on both. I considered myself lucky to pass at all, since I hadn't studied much.

On the last day of class Hooper let us go early. She told us she had twelve potlucks to attend over the holidays. She wore tight blue jeans and a sleeveless turtleneck and hugged each one of us as we left the room, even a cringing Jeremy. She smelled of ponderosa pine, her seasonal perfume.

Although my family hadn't exchanged presents at Christmas for years, I had Nan teach me how to knit so I could make Billy a toque and a scarf. It took me forever. I even wove in a T + B in silver thread.

He unwrapped his gift on Hill 5 and draped the scarf around his neck.

"How do I look?"

I tightened the scarf. "What about the toque?"

"It'll mess up my hair."

"So you'd rather freeze your ears off."

He reached for the toque and I adjusted it on his head.

"Now you're ready for a squall," I told him.

He'd made me truffles coated in gold leaf. The chocolates were infused with lavender and ginger. I tied the velvet ribbon they were wrapped in to my braid.

Then he passed me another small box. Inside it was an expensive-looking compact digital camera. I knew I'd never use it.

"There's a couple pictures in there already," he told me.

I powered it on and a photo of a glass condo on a beach appeared.

"Dad says that's ours if I get into California State and go part-time. You can work on the website and take bookings when I'm in class." He hit the arrow, to two matching monogrammed surfboards, apparently ready and waiting for us in his garage.

He kissed my earlobe, neck and hands as I watched tanker trucks going up and down the roads within the Air Force grid.

Life with Billy was going to be fun. The catering business would involve hard work and long nights, but he'd make me delicacies that melted in my mouth. And we'd surf. While he was studying, I'd go up and down the California coast with my camera and the shots would come easily.

I'd never have to think about the wars and missiles and End Times ever again.

Despite Angstrom's many landing strips and planes, Halo was too small to have its own airport, so Nan and I drove the Airstream to Shady Springs to pick Mom up. Nan never wanted to use the truck anymore. She only took the Airstream, even around town, to practice her driving.

There were patches of black ice on the highway. Nan drove below the speed limit and played Leonard Cohen the whole way there.

She'd met him at a laundromat in Calgary. She was in her early twenties and hadn't met Grandpa Wallace yet. Cohen was on tour, almost famous, but he still did his own washing. While they waited for their clothes to dry they went to the diner next door and had a cup of coffee.

"You should have stolen his underwear. You could have made a fortune on eBay," I told her.

She shushed me as the next song came on. Cohen was harmonizing with some lady about scars on a dark green hill — *So my body leaves no scars on you ...*

I thought about Gabriel Finch and his scars. The ones I hadn't seen. When an image of his naked body flashed through my mind I willed it away and blamed it on Leonard.

As soon as we entered the airport we could see Mom weaving through the crowd at Arrivals. Her coat was made of blue fun fur. She wore moon boots, and her arms were loaded with bags. Even though she was still inside, big sunglasses took up half her face.

She looked completely insane.

"Charlie!" Nan called and waved.

Mom ran toward us, dropped her bags and brought us both into her arms, practically choking me.

"Let me look at you." She pushed me back. "You're too thin, Twinkles. Are you eating?"

"The girl eats like a horse," Nan said.

There was a shiny green fleck stuck to Mom's nostril.

"Did you get your nose pierced?" I asked.

"You like?" Then her hand was at my throat, pulling the whistle out from under my hoodie. "Good. You're still wearing it."

We helped her with her things and started the long drive back to Halo. Mom barely stopped for a breath the whole way. It was times like these that I wished she had a Pause button.

Nan had more patience. She listened and nodded, eyes on the road. "That's great, Charlie. Good for you. Sounds promising."

Mom was fidgety and wound up. She didn't ask about Dad. Instead she ran her hand along the bench's flamingo fabric and looked around the Airstream. When she spotted *Twilight's Last Gleaming* she bee-lined for the canvas. She'd probably expected to find it hanging in my room.

"You sure snazzed the van up, Nancy," she finally said, straightening the painting. "A gal could practically live in here." She came and sat beside me again. "So. Update me."

"Dad'll be home."

"I know."

"You talked?"

"Texted. He didn't reply. So I figure he's fine with my being here."

Nan gave a snort. "We'll soon find out."

Mom twisted her rings. She had them on every finger, even her thumbs. A ring with a turquoise stone had replaced her wedding band. Another was amber and the others, wood and pewter and glass.

Her hands were spotless, which meant she hadn't been painting.

We passed horses and ranches and cattle. We passed a wind farm with white steel windmills lined up like crosses in a military cemetery.

"Have you thought about where you'll apply in January?" Mom asked. She and Nan had both been on my case about colleges.

"Can't afford it."

"Payment plans or student loans is how most people do it, darlin'. Or scholarships if you feel inclined to improve your grades."

When I didn't respond she changed the subject. "How's Billy?"

"He's in Chicago. Gabriel Finch is coming to lunch."

Mom caught Nan's eye in the rearview mirror.

"What?" I said, irritated.

"Nothing, Twinks." She put her hand on my knee. "I'd like to hear all about your volunteer work."

I considered telling them what had happened to Gabriel in town, then decided against it. Mom would insist I stay away from him, and I wasn't about to do that. Anyway, she forfeited her right to tell me what to do when she left us.

18

Dad came home on Christmas Eve. The first thing he did was look around the bungalow, like he expected to find Mom there.

"She's at Jackie's, Emmett," Nan said from the kitchen, where she was following a turkey-stuffing video. We'd already made the cranberry sauce, also by video instruction. Mom was the one who used to prepare our holiday dinners and I was excited about having a meal together again as a family, even if we were a broken one.

Dad came back into the kitchen, got a beer from the fridge and cracked it open.

"When's lunch tomorrow?"

"Noon."

"You're really cooking?"

"What's it look like?" She raised her hands covered in bread, onion and celery.

I joined him at the table.

"So. You think it'll happen?" he asked Nan.

"Do I think what will happen?"

"Angstrom."

"Seems that way."

It was our hometown, after all. I knew that Nan would take

off in her silver bullet but I had no idea what Dad would do.

"Most'll move to Shady Springs," Dad said, resigned. "Guess we'll go there, too."

"We're not sheep," I told him. "We don't have to follow everyone. Why not start over someplace new?"

"I don't want to start over."

I was in no mood for Dad's pity party. I put on my boots, got my coat and told them I was going shopping with Mom.

"Drop me off at Reg's," Dad said, finishing his beer, grabbing another from the fridge and putting on his Storm Rider.

"And you'll be back tomorrow," I said.

He belched. "Precisely."

"Don't get wasted."

"Come again?"

"Don't show up wasted. In case you hadn't noticed, we're putting a lot of effort into this."

Nan watched us, knife in hand, not saying a word.

On Christmas morning we put the turkey in the oven, then cleaned the Brussels sprouts and boiled some potatoes. We pushed two tables together in the living room and set them with a long lace cloth. Nan brought out some chipped china and crystal goblets.

Shortly after, Mom, Jackie and Jolene arrived.

Mom wore a low-cut black dress and she had her hair in an upsweep. Her lips matched her fake ruby jewelry and I held my breath as she came in. She looked stunning. She'd bought the dress at Ajax Outlets, along with a lot of other stuff on credit.

She'd insisted on buying me a pricey dress, too, in a color she called cobalt.

"It's important for a gal to have something swanky on hand in case a special occasion arises," she'd told me. As soon as I got home I shoved it into the back of the closet.

For luncheon I wore jeans and the new T-shirt I'd treated myself to at the outlets, made from soft cotton the same purple as my boots.

Jolene and Jackie were done up in a mother-daughter ensemble, sequined and gaudy. They came in chattering as the doorbell went again.

When I opened the door, Jeremy Colt stood before me. He wore a Santa hat and pressed a wilted poinsettia against my chest as he stepped inside.

"Why are you here?" I asked.

"Your mom invited me at Jo's."

So he'd ditched his own dad on Christmas. It was common knowledge that Mr. Colt never left the house and was drugged up on antidepressants. But it didn't give Jeremy the right to ruin my holiday.

Nan came up behind me.

"Come in," she told him, taking his coat.

"Merry Christmas, Missus Lee." Jeremy smiled.

"He's not invited," I told Nan, not caring that he could hear me.

Nan grabbed my arm and pulled me aside. "Come now, Twyla. Where are your manners? Add another place at the table."

I added a wobbly bench next to Jolene's seat. Mom kept glancing at the door and at her watch. Then Trav and Carm arrived with a plate of homemade churros.

While everyone was making small talk, I slipped out to get Gabriel.

Before leaving I checked myself in the mirror by the front

door. I put on some lip gloss Mom had bought me, pulled out my braid and twisted my hair into a messy bun.

Driving through Halo I rolled my window down and caught whiffs of turkey coming from the houses and apartment blocks. Kids played hockey on homemade ponds. Churches were full. Families sledded and built forts.

Even if we had enough nukes under our land to blow up the world, on this day our town was like a Norman Rockwell painting.

Gabriel was outside with Storm when I got to the farm. They were running around in the snow, and when I approached he threw a snowball at me.

"Seriously?" I said, throwing one back. Then my phone dinged.

Happy Christmas Pocahontas.

I wrote hastily. *Peeling yams. Call you later.*

I had no idea why I lied.

Miss you, Billy's last text read.

I shoved the phone deep into my coat pocket. Gabriel took an ax from the porch and we went to a wooded area off the property. We walked for a bit without talking until he sat on a log by a frozen stream, and I sat next to him.

"We used to cut our tree here every year," he said. "Elsie always picked it out."

"I'm sorry about your sister," I told him, wishing I could think of something meaningful to say.

He looked up at the treetops. "That's one of my last memories of her ..." His voice drifted. He took a stick and drew in the snow with it. "Anyway, let's do this."

We walked to a patch of trees lit by the sun and chose one with full, silvery-green needles. I breathed in and smelled it, then stuck my hand through the branches and held it while

Gabriel chopped. Then we dragged the fir to the truck and tied it down with bungee cords, locked Storm in the house and made our way back to Ash Crescent.

After we brought the tree inside and put it in the stand, I introduced Gabriel to everyone except Dad, who hadn't come home the night before. Jeremy was the only one who didn't get up to shake his hand. Instead he smirked and gave a salute from the couch.

I took a few pictures with my phone as proof that Gabriel was with us, and sent them to Lucinda. Then Carm, Travis and I decorated the tree.

Jeremy whistled from the couch. "You oughta stick your silver star up top," he told Gabriel, who sat across from him. "Except you don't have one."

"Damn straight," Gabriel told Jeremy. "Can't say I ever received a medal for gallantry in action."

He left the living room and went into the hallway.

I poured some eggnog and went over to where he was studying a few of my photos that Nan had framed. The pictures were shots of town reflected in puddles of water.

I handed him a cup.

"These yours?" he asked.

"Yep," I told him.

"You don't take yourself seriously." His eyes were steady on me. "You should."

A strange feeling rose in my chest. "How's the cut?"

He touched the crooked bandage on his forehead. "Good as gone."

When the turkey was ready he helped Nan carve it. Then we

all put our heads down and Jackie Bolton said grace.

I sat beside Gabriel. He was the first one to compliment Nan on the cooking. Everyone else shoveled the food in but he ate slowly and deliberately, breathing deeply after each bite. I watched him relax in his chair.

Then Dad walked in. He'd combed his hair and he wore a pressed shirt and clean jeans, and his boots were polished. He must have gotten ready at Reg's place. Before taking his seat he nodded at everyone including Mom, and all through lunch he stared at her across the table.

Mom turned to Gabriel. "Twyla tells me you're busy on the farm," she smiled, taking a sip of wine.

"With a *mosaic*," Jeremy snarled and didn't look up from his plate.

My face went hot as Gabriel stared at me. I glanced from Jeremy to Jolene, trying to understand what had just happened.

"Billy told me," Jolene mouthed apologetically.

"A mosaic?" Mom asked.

"Promoting the terrorists," Jeremy added.

"Don't be a moron, Jeremy. It's scenes from before the wars. Of this place called Uruk," I tried explaining to everyone. "In the silo."

Then I turned to Mom. "I thought we'd enter it in the MoMA contest."

"What's MoMA?" Jolene asked me.

"The Museum of Modern Art. In New York City."

"My contest?" Mom asked.

"Yeah."

She laughed a bit too loud. "I think that's a great idea. I'd love to see it."

Dad reached for the gravy boat.

"It's like those cathedrals in your art books," I told Nan.

"What did you say these pictures were ... portraying?" Nan asked.

Gabriel put his napkin on the table and stared at his lap.

"I had a friend," he started. "Who used to tell me stories. About life before the invasions."

"It's the Middle East in ancient times," I cut in.

"Tell them what it's made from," Jeremy said, giving Gabriel a black look.

Gabriel glanced at everyone at the table. "Ammo."

Jeremy let his cutlery drop so that it clanked against his plate. He wiped his mouth and grimaced. "Instead of using it the way you should be, to protect our country, you're making skeezy pictures glorifying *them*. The hostiles. You might as well say it."

"Say what?"

"You don't believe in our cause."

"That's cold, man," Gabriel told him. "I'm saying sometimes I wonder if ..."

"If what?" Mom urged.

"If we made things worse." His voice had gone hard.

Mom nodded. Jeremy gave a maniacal laugh.

"Ask your dad," Gabriel told him.

"Leave him out of it. He's not the one siding with the sand monkeys."

Gabriel looked around at everyone. "We're partly to blame for the shape these territories are in. No wonder they hate us."

Jeremy slammed a fist down, knocking over a glass. Gabriel's hands curled around a rifle that wasn't there. As they lunged at each other from across the table, Nan stood up and so did Dad.

"They're not hostiles, dirtbag," Gabriel said, grabbing hold of Jeremy's wrists. "It's racists like you who give our country a bad name."

"Way I heard it you hosed 'em all anyway," Jeremy said as he tried to squirm out of Gabriel's wristlock. He whipped an arm free. "Way I heard it, you —"

Gabriel pushed him and Jeremy went flying into the tree, bringing it crashing down.

"That's enough," Nan said, while Dad blocked Jeremy from attacking Gabriel. "This is worse than the classroom. I've a good mind to shove both your heads in a snow bank."

Jolene twirled a piece of hair around her finger while Jackie helped herself to seconds. Carm made the sign of the cross and whispered something to Travis.

Mom muttered to Jackie, "Sounds too political to me. Can't see him winning."

I put a hand on Gabriel's arm and led him away from the table.

"Scram," Nan ordered. "Go get some air."

"Thank you for the meal," Gabriel said dismally.

I grabbed our coats and forced him out the door.

"I didn't think Billy would say anything," I told him. "This is my fault."

"It's done. Forget about it," he said. "It's a small town. I knew this would be the reaction." He shook his head. "I shouldn't have said all that."

"Jeremy's a punk. It's good you set him straight."

I took my skates and Dad's from the garage, and we drove to the river. By the time we got there, I noticed the shakes in Gabriel's hands. But I refused to drive him home until we'd gone onto the ice.

It was a sunny afternoon and there were a lot of people out. I didn't recognize anyone and was relieved.

Some stealth bombers passed overhead, flying in a V-formation like geese. The planes released streams of green and red smoke as they veered off toward the mountains and everyone oohed and aahed.

"I know Jeremy's full of shit," I said, lacing up, "but did something bad happen? Did someone die?"

"Are you kidding me?" Gabriel looked at the bombers then at me like I was clueless. "Hundreds die there every day, Twyla. No one cares. We lose one of ours and it's a goddamn travesty and we up the airstrikes."

"I'm confused. How do you really feel about the wars?"

"I believe before we invaded, terrorist groups didn't exist the way they do now. I also believe we wouldn't be so involved in these missions if there was no oil there."

"Then why keep fighting?"

He bent down to tighten his laces. When he looked at me again, his face was unreadable. "We were supposed to bring peace. That's why." He sounded tired. He pressed his hands on his jeans to steady them before we stepped onto the ice.

Gabriel skated like a hockey player, fast and smooth. It took me a while to catch up and maneuver my way beside him. As we glided along, the cold air brightened his cheeks. Sometimes he turned and faced me, skating backward. I had a hard time keeping up with him.

Afterwards we bought hot chocolate and rested on a bench in the warming hut to watch the other skaters.

He stared out at the frozen expanse as it started to snow.

"This winding river of ours," he said. "Seems mythic somehow."

"Slop River? Not my first thought."

"The Greeks claimed that after you died your soul went down to the underworld. You paid a ferryman to cross rivers dividing the world of the living from the world of the dead. Then you stopped at a cave and drank from the river there, and your soul forgot life on earth."

"Cool."

"The cave of forgetting. If you believe in that sort of thing." Gabriel studied me. He rubbed his hands together, then tucked them into his coat pockets. "Aside from Rambo back at the house, this was the nicest Christmas I've had in years."

19

After I dropped Gabriel off at the farm I saw that I'd missed several calls from Billy.

Why did you tell Jolene? I texted.

She said Jeremy said we were building bombs in there. That's why.

You shouldn't have told her.

Whatever.

Now everyone knows. It caused a fight between Jeremy and Gabriel at lunch.

Why was he at your lunch?

Because I invited him, I wrote, and shoved my phone back into my pocket.

Our guests were gone when I got to the house, except for Mom who was at the sink with Dad, doing dishes.

Nan stopped me at the door.

"We need to talk," she said. The three of them had probably drawn straws to figure out who'd do the lecturing.

I followed Nan into the living room and sat down next to her.

"Tell me if I've got this straight. Gabriel Finch is making a mosaic in the decommissioned silo on the farm property. From ammunition."

"You got it."

"And he's entering it in an art contest."

"I convinced him. His family's broke. They'll lose the farm."

"This is what you're volunteering for."

I nodded.

"Are the Help a Vet folks aware of the project?" she asked.

"Why? What's he done wrong?"

"Same way as someone who's not a soldier dressing up as a soldier is a crime, some might see this as defacing Air Force property."

"He's not defacing it. What he's making is … it's breathtaking."

"That may be how you perceive it but others won't feel that way. For starters, Halo's bumper-sticker crowd."

She meant the townies who drove around with *If You Don't Stand Behind Our Troops You're Welcome to Stand in Front of Them* plastered on their vehicles.

I knew Mom and Dad were listening to every word by how quietly they washed and dried.

I took Nan's hand. "I'm contributing to something important," I said. "I believe in what he's doing."

"My, my. And what happened to your anti-war sentiments?"

"His art's promoting peace. He's not a Marine anymore."

"Once a Marine, always a Marine."

"But I'm starting to get that a lot of these guys enlist because they want to help."

Nan sighed. "War changes people. Circumstances make them capable of atrocities."

"You're saying everyone who goes over does bad things?"

"I'm telling you that something's marked that boy."

Mom and Dad came into the living room then.

"We don't want you getting emotionally involved, Twy," Mom said. "We're worried you'll get hurt."

They looked like they felt sorry for me.

"You think I've got a crush on an unstable vet?" I asked. "Well, I don't. So quit riding my ass."

They kept right on with their pity looks. So I said I had a headache and wished them goodnight. And that was how Christmas ended.

Mom stayed at Jackie Bolton's for the rest of the week, but each day she stopped in to spend time with us. She and Dad got along fine. So much so that I felt like I was Mom's excuse to see Dad. They sat together on the couch a lot, Dad playing his guitar, Mom humming. They even ate meals together and watched movies. But after Dad went back on rotation, Mom mostly took naps. She didn't ask to see the mosaic again, and she left us on New Year's Eve.

I hadn't seen Gabriel since Christmas and wanted to wish him a happy New Year, so I detoured to the Finch property on my way home from my shift at Tomahawk. The mall was dead and Travis had let me go early.

I pulled up at the farm and walked through the fresh blanket of snow covering the fields. The door was unlocked so I let myself in. I could hear him on the phone with Lucinda.

"Yes, I'm eating. She's here right now. Stop yelling. I can hear you. Love you, too, Mom."

There were crates of ammo on the floor from different warehouses. Looking at the cartridge boxes, I wondered what new images Gabriel had in mind, although most of the wall space was already covered.

As he hung up I sat beside him on the couch, where Storm lay at his feet.

There were some sketches on the coffee table. Stone walls, a fountain, a spire with a rounded tip.

"Warhead?" I asked.

"Minaret. Used for the call to prayer."

I'd heard about the recordings played through loudspeakers. "Did the chanting drive you nuts?"

"I stopped noticing it after a while. Now I hear it in my sleep." His hands rested in his lap. The tremor was there again.

I ran a finger along the coffee table between the beer cans and the ashtray, picking up a layer of grit. I'd only cleaned a few times since September and it was starting to show.

"Dusty in here," I said.

"You don't know dust."

I picked up on his cue. "Right. Because you were in the sandbox."

He sank deeper into the couch.

"There was a major storm when I first got there," he told me. "A shamal. This violent wind that makes depressions in the dunes. The blowing sand stripped paint off cars. If you got it in the face it made your skin bleed. You breathed the dust in for weeks after." He paused. "This little boy told me through our translator once, how the desert sands sing. Apparently they sound mournful."

"Like the wind in the cornfields?"

"Don't know. I never heard any song."

"Did you patrol and guard the streets?" I asked. "Is that what you did there?"

"We dug up wells. And IEDs. Filled potholes. Blew things up. Manned checkpoints and took supplies places. That about sums it up."

"What did you do on New Year's Eve?"

He shrugged. "Ate in the chow hall. Surfed the web. Worked out."

Then he laughed.

"What?"

"When we were bored we made videos of camel spiders."

"Camel spiders?"

"There's urban legends about them. Like, that they eat camel stomachs and take chunks out of soldiers and chase after anything human."

"Gross."

"Their bites hurt like hell but they're not poisonous. Or even that big. They run fast because they're running from the sun. They're night creatures. Fragile, when you look up close. They'll hunt you for your shadow. That's all."

"And you videoed them?"

"We screwed around with the footage to make them, like, up to your knees huge. Turned them into beasts. Everyone back home believed what we posted. Then we made a show of destroying them with our boots." He shook his head. "Weird thing is, at night they run toward light."

"I don't get it."

"Me neither. Except, maybe …" He frowned.

"Maybe what?"

"Maybe they're like those of us in these wars. Gunning it into darkness, then trying to get back into the light. Only we can't."

We both stayed quiet for a minute.

"Are their webs big?" I asked.

He smiled. "They make nests. Lined with hair. That they clip from your head while you sleep."

He reached out and touched my hair, which gave my heart a skip.

"They'd have a heyday with yours," he told me.

I replied without thinking. "So when you weren't killing people you were killing animals."

He moved away so fast it was like I'd slapped him.

Part of me was joking around, but I kept remembering the incident in town and what Jeremy had said.

Then there was the mosaic. And the person I was getting to know, not as a Marine but as someone who seemed good, and wise, and different from anyone I'd ever met.

"I didn't mean it like that," I said. "Just tell me what went on that seems to be making everyone so mad."

He stood and paced. "Telling you won't change the outcome. I'm not going to talk about it, Twyla."

Outside at barely five o'clock the sun was setting. I invited him to come with me to Ash Crescent but he said he had to get back to work. I thought about the small celebration that most of Halo would attend later downtown. There would be fireworks and the wind would carry the sound through the farmlands. Gabriel would hear the blasts and probably think only of gunfire.

Later on, after Nan and I watched *The English Patient*, our annual tradition, and after we rang in the New Year, I fell asleep and had a dream.

In my dream the Great Plains had dried up into a wasteland and life as we knew it had ended. We lived in an underground bunker with a viewing room. A cinema with clips of the outdoors and nature as it once was. We rationed our water like gold and a machine with buttons gave off scents of the Gone World, like the peppery smell of wild roses and the sweet perfume of coulees on the plain.

Nan, Mom and Dad, and Billy were there but I couldn't find Gabriel. His mosaic was gone, too. I looked through a porthole window where I saw flaming birds dropping from the air, landing in black water. The sky glowed and I was so, so thirsty.

Then his voice called my name and I woke up.

20

I spent the last of my vacation at the farm. The contest deadline was less than two weeks away. Gabriel had finished a section with an orchard, as well as a portrait of a shepherd with some goats. I never complained about the cold inside the silo, but when he brought in a couple of space heaters, I knew he'd done it for me.

I was a pro now at sorting through the ammo. Although carting buckets of metal was backbreaking, when I was organizing and counting I didn't worry about Billy or California or what the wars had done to Gabriel, and I didn't get stressed about Mom and Dad, or Halo being decommissioned.

Each time I walked down the ramp and into the dome, the mosaic left me breathless. At the same time, I wondered what Gabriel would do once his masterpiece was finished. It seemed to be what kept him going.

He didn't like wasting time taking breaks and I couldn't stomach MREs. So both days I spent with him, I filled Nan's picnic basket with turkey sandwiches and nachos from Taco John's, and we sat on my blanket and listened to Hank Williams while we ate.

I kept hoping that Gabriel would open up about what had happened in the wars. I wondered if he'd made some horrible mistake. Occasionally we heard stories about how the military accidentally killed the people they were supposed to protect. My new strategy was to try to find out through general, harmless questions.

"What did you do at night over there?" I asked as I passed him a bag of chips.

"Sleep."

I gave an exaggerated sigh. "I mean when you weren't sleeping."

"Didn't have many nights off."

"But when you did."

"Played knucklebones. Bet against myself."

"How do you play?"

"Toss anklebones from goats or sheep, like dice. Each side's worth a different number. You try to add up to whatever number's in your head."

"Then what?"

"Then nothing. It's a dumb, random game. There's no meaning in it." He reached for some cartridges and tossed them into the air. "Or you throw the bones up one by one and catch them on the backs of your hands."

The cartridges fell onto my boots. I licked my thumb and rubbed at the soft leather.

"You really think these are shitty-ass?" I asked him.

"I'm crazy about your boots, Twyla," he replied.

My throat tightened.

He lay down and put his arms behind his head and stared up at the ceiling. I stretched out, too, to take it all in: the golds, silvers and bronzes of this legendary world that Gabriel was creating. I imagined what it would be like when the ceiling was removed and the light filtered in. I proposed a glass roof, so things wouldn't get damaged. Gabriel lit up at that idea.

We were discussing the specifics of it when I heard talking coming from the tunnel. We hadn't locked the blast door. Lately Gabriel had been keeping it open a crack to let in fresh air, and because it was so heavy to move.

The voices got louder and soon enough, Jeremy Colt, Jake Pritchett, Troy Whitman and Michael Kemp were at the entrance to the dome, each of them holding a flashlight. They looked at the mosaic panels and tried to hide their astonishment.

"So this is what's got Twyla's panties in a knot," Jeremy said. "This is why she rushes out at bell while that poor sucker Billy chases after her like a dog."

Troy and Michael chuckled. Only Jake seemed like he didn't want to be there.

Jeremy slid some chew under his lip, sucked it back and spat on the ground.

Gabriel whistled for Storm but the dog didn't come.

"Don't bother," Jeremy told him. "We tied your pooch up good."

Gabriel got up and held a hand out for me to do the same.

"Stay here," he said. He walked over to Jeremy and gave him a hard, unblinking stare. "This is private property."

Jeremy's eyes scanned the space and landed back on Gabriel as he cracked his knuckles. They were about the same height but Jeremy was bulkier.

"Think you deserve to stick around here after what you've done?" he said.

"Chill, dude," Jake told Jeremy, stepping in to pull him back. But by then Gabriel had Jeremy by the throat and was pushing him against the wall.

"Get out," he told Jeremy in a whisper, releasing him. Jeremy coughed and leaned forward to catch his breath before eyeing Gabriel once more. The veins at his temples bulged and his nostrils flared.

The other guys started walking away. As Jeremy moved back toward the tunnel, he yelled, "Heard it all. About how you blazed 'em." He grabbed his crotch and whistled, his laughter echoing back at us.

Once they were gone, Gabriel sat down and put his head between his knees.

"Twyla, you need to go," he said in a barely controlled voice.

I put a hand on his back but he didn't react. Knowing how when I said I wanted to be alone I meant it, I left.

The next day when I pulled up at the farm, there was a Humvee the color of desert sand there. Someone was finally following through with the spot-checking.

Through the dirty porch window I watched two uniformed Marines sitting in the living room while Gabriel paced around.

A middle-aged man with a square jaw and a thick neck was talking, but I couldn't hear what he was saying. The muscles in his face moved when he spoke. His knees came practically to his shoulders as he sat on the couch, and he leafed through forms on a clipboard, probably asking Gabriel about my hours. The other guy was a lot younger, a thin and jumpy kid. He had a leg that wouldn't stop shaking and he swiveled around the room a lot.

When Storm caught sight of me and started barking, they all looked my way so I let myself in.

"Hi!" I said, a little too pumped up. The Marines stood to go.

"Miss your sorry ass, Finchy," the smaller guy said.

"Good seeing you, Rolo," Gabriel replied.

"Keep the dialogue open," Muscle Face told him. They nodded politely when they passed by me, and I nodded back.

"I'm Twyla Jane Lee, putting in my time for Help a Vet. But I suppose you've already noted that." I pointed to the clipboard.

"Beg your pardon?" Muscle Face paused.

"Help a Vet. Hawthorn High's partnership with your volunteer program."

"Gotcha," Rolo smiled. Then he saluted Gabriel. "Later, Finchy."

Gabriel went over to the window and watched them drive away.

"You know them?"

"We go back. Same platoon."

"Talk about a coincidence that they're on Help a Vet now," I said. "What are the odds?"

He seemed preoccupied. He put on his coat and I had to run to keep up with him as we headed to the silo.

"Should we discuss what happened yesterday?" I asked.

"Nothing to discuss."

I didn't push it. Because this was exactly what Jeremy wanted — to plant lies and doubt in my mind where Gabriel was concerned.

"We need to get going on the contest application. Deadline's coming up. I scanned the photos," I told him. "They're ready to go. Want to see?"

"I'm sure they're fine."

"You'll need to fill out the questionnaire."

"How 'bout you do it." He glanced back at me as he pulled the blast door open.

"The questions are personal."

"Just put whatever."

I changed my tactic. "Have you ever been to MoMA?" I asked as we walked down the ramp.

"Not that I recall."

"If you make top three you get to go."

"How's that?"

"It's part of the prize. Plus, if you win, your work goes on display."

"This isn't transportable."

"They'd video it or something."

"I'm not a fan of cities."

"It's one of the most famous museums in the world. What if I go with you?"

By then we were in the dome, and he was turning on the lights.

"In that case we'd better get to work."

He led me to the base of the ramp, where he'd begun geometrically tiling the concrete ground. I knelt and felt the cold, smooth metals rippling under my fingers in a key pattern.

"It's called tessellation," Gabriel told me as he knelt beside me.

I looked around, discouraged. "You're planning on doing the whole floor, aren't you."

"And the ramp." He grinned. "Added bonus. Seeing as you want to get to New York so bad."

I groaned. "We'll never finish in time."

"You don't need it for the submission," he told me. "C'mon, Lee. Improvise. Adapt. Overcome."

21

I completed the artist questionnaire as best as I could. I loaded up my pictures and submitted the entry package just before the deadline.

Billy was back from Chicago but we hadn't seen each other much outside of school. I'd picked up extra shifts at Taco John's, and Martin Goodwin had locked him away at Affinity to work on college applications.

He came by when he first got home, full of apologies for telling Jolene about the mosaic. I was still furious with him. But then he kept saying how sorry he was and he looked broken up about it. When he kissed me I couldn't stay mad.

The big school trip was happening soon, so he was being extra attentive. He even grabbed me in the hall a few times and pressed me up against the lockers, which made my head spin.

Since the contest submission was done, Gabriel said he wanted to take a break and recharge. I still stopped by so we could sort through casings and clean stuff up, but like Nan and Mom, he pushed me to get studying and deal with university deadlines. So during the weeks before leaving for Yellowstone I focused on my own applications for college to shut Gabriel and my family up. I didn't plan on going but applied to the liberal arts programs at California State, UCLA and UC Berkeley.

I also told Dad I wouldn't be going anywhere in-state, and I told him about my plans with Billy. He barely reacted. "I guess it's your life," he said on the phone.

I got my recommendation letter from Dodge, who wrote the same things for all his students. My essay talked about Grandpa Wallace and how his photography inspired me. I also threw in a few pictures of the mosaic to show that I worked as an art assistant. But my test scores weren't high enough and I had no extracurriculars. I wasn't college material and I knew it.

The day we left town I texted Gabriel. *Headed to Yellowstone, back Friday.* I wasn't sure what else to say. He knew about the annual trip. He would have taken it himself as a student.

Bon voyage, was all he wrote back.

On the long ride to the national park, Hooper tried to get some songs going. But we were all plugged in, tuned out, headphones on, and she soon gave up.

Jeremy and Jolene had opted out of the trip. It was a relief to be away from Jeremy. And his goons at the back of the bus were quieter without him.

"Check this," Billy said, scrolling his phone. "Who's a volcano's favorite singer?"

"Who," I replied, looking out the window as daylight spread across the snowy plains and through the utility corridors.

"Johnny Ash."

"Funny."

"What's a volcano's favorite historical document?"

"Don't know."

"The Magma Carta."

I sighed.

"Actually there's no supervolcano in Yellowstone. Chuck Norris is just having a barbecue."

He tried to tickle me but I pushed his hand away.

He looked down at my camera. "Why aren't you using the new one?"

"I am," I lied. "But I didn't want it to get trashed."

I adjusted the Leica around my neck and held it in close. I'd managed to take a few pictures of Gabriel the last time we'd worked on tiling the floor, shooting from the hip so he wouldn't notice. That same roll of film was still inside the camera. Gabriel's undeveloped image was there on the bus with me.

While Billy played video games I went onto the contest site. Public voting had begun. Six hundred and ninety-two entries had been vetted, approved and posted through an initial screening process. Gradually the works with the lowest number of votes would be eliminated until there were just ten left. Then the judges would assess the top entries and chose the winner.

It took me a while to find our submission. I scrolled through sculptures, paintings, videos and mixed-media installations. There was also a lot of performance and graffiti art.

The mosaic was on page 19 of 20. My black-and-white photographs looked dull compared to all the other brightly colored pictures.

Some profiles were five pages long and the artist statements were full of highfalutin' words like hermeneutic, nihilism, semiotic, atemporal and ideology. Ours just read: *Installation, decommissioned nuclear missile silo, Montana. Materials: cartridges and casings. Date made: Ongoing. Title: Halo Mosaic. Artist: Gabriel Finch.*

The entry was in the lower third quadrant, with twenty-seven votes and zero likes or comments.

It hit me then that Gabriel could be eliminated in the first round.

I looked for Mom's painting but couldn't find it. When I texted her and asked, she said she'd changed her mind about the contest. She was tired of being an artist. She was starting up a health-juice business instead.

I stared out the window again and tried to spot all of the silos in the barren fields.

Angstrom had fired a test missile a few days before. The Air Force did this four times a year from different locations across the country. Officials flew over from Washington on what was called a Glory Trip and there was a special dinner beforehand. The missile squadron launched the rocket at 3:54 a.m. local time and it landed on target in Guam forty minutes later.

Outside there was a countdown. Sightseers watched from bleachers a few miles from the launch site. As the rocket blasted off, everyone posted and tweeted videos and selfies. The *Interceptor* quoted the witnesses, who said, "Majestic!", "Annihilate 'em!", "Bam!" and "This is how we win!"

I wondered what our last sunrise would look like. Would it be different from other sunrises? Would it linger like the last breath of a dying person saying, *Goodbye world. Goodbye, goodbye, goodbye.*

After unloading at the lodge, we went snowshoeing. Hooper and Dodge were our escorts along with a hired guide.

As we started along the trail, snow began to fall, like someone had flipped a switch to pretty up the scene. On the loop back, the guide led us to a firepit. By then it was early evening. The sky had cleared and the constellations were coming out. Then we saw a meteor, this fireball traveling through space and time. We watched the bright streak and made wishes.

"Tell me yours so we don't double up," Billy said. "I'll go for the beachfront condo."

I wished that Gabriel Finch would win America's Next Great Artist.

"World peace," I told him.

It was a perfect, romantic night. Yet when Billy held me close and whispered how much he loved me again, I couldn't say it back.

At the lodge our guide gave us a talk with a film on the Yellowstone Caldera, the biggest supervolcano in North America. She told us the volcano was active, and that there were thousands of earthquakes in the park every year, most so small you couldn't feel them.

When the presentation was over, Hooper took a headcount and passed around the next day's itinerary. Everyone scattered to the dorms and I followed Billy down the corridor to his room, where he let himself in, then gave me his key.

I returned to the bunk I shared with Crystal Jones and waited an hour until she was snoring. I broke into a sweat as I tiptoed out to Billy's room and slipped into his cot. He'd thrown his blue T-shirt over the bedside lamp so the small space glowed like we were under the ocean. He'd already placed a condom on the nightstand.

I straddled him and we were charged like static electricity, sparking against each other. He knew just what to do to light me up. I pulled my shirt off and unbuckled his belt. He flipped me down and was over me and we kissed each other all over, and he did a lot of moaning and groping.

But the more we made out, the more my mind wandered.

I saw our future together, a carefree life in the sun with lots of parties and friends. Then I thought about Gabriel, this person who seemed to be in as many pieces as his mosaic. I never knew what he was thinking. It was exhausting. Yet there was something about him that calmed me, the same way that the Big Open calmed me. All I wanted to do was get back to the farm. Back to where he was.

I felt like I was suffocating. I pushed Billy off.

"I can't," I told him.

He rubbed his face and ran a hand through his hair as we both sat up.

"What's wrong?" he asked.

I reached for my hoodie and jeans. "I'm not sure."

Billy's voice hardened. "It's him, isn't it."

I shook my head.

"Look at me, Twyla."

I faced him, a lump in my throat. "I'm sorry, Billy." I didn't know what else to say.

"Which part are you sorry about?"

"Just … everything."

"Don't let him wreck our plans, Twy. He'll ruin your life."

"I can't even swim."

"What?"

"I don't like water. What would I do in California?"

"Be with me," he said, his voice thick with hurt.

"Follow you."

"That was the idea."

"What about my dreams?"

"You don't have any."

Billy grabbed his jeans and reached for his T-shirt and suddenly the room was too bright.

He paced the rickety space, the floor creaking. Then he punched the wall so hard that his fist put a dent in the wood paneling. I worried Hooper would hear us. He'd never been violent before and I didn't like it.

I got up to go. When he tried to grab my arm I stepped back. Then he blocked the door.

"Get out of my way, Billy."

He moved in closer. "You want me to enlist? Is that it?"

"Don't be like that."

"Because what you're saying is, I'm no match for him."

"That's not true."

His shoulders went up and down in time with his breathing. He finally stepped aside and dropped his head.

"Then why?"

"I just don't think … we're a match for each other."

"He's a Marine, Twyla. He kills people for a living."

"Gabriel's trying to get a message out. About the wars."

"He's relieving his guilty conscience, dragging you down with him. I give it a year before you quit taking pictures and he ditches you and you're stuck at Taco John's until you're forty, when you have a nervous breakdown like your mom."

"There's no need to be cruel," I told him.

He opened the door for me to leave.

"I'm going to tell you something for your own good," he said. "You know what always bugged me? You think you're different from everyone. But you're not. You'll end up alone."

And maybe Billy was right. While everyone around me coupled up, I waded alone in the mineral mists of the local hot springs. And I rode alone on our field trip to Old Faithful, as Billy hung out at the back of the snow coach. I cross-country skied alone, trailing behind the group in an area near the geysers. All the scenic stops in the country's oldest national park I experienced alone, without Billy, who avoided me for the rest of the trip.

144

I also sat alone on the drive back to Halo. Everyone was quiet from lack of sleep, until our vehicle made a sharp, sudden pull onto the snowy shoulder.

The driver didn't say anything, but I caught his eyes widening in the rearview mirror.

I heard it before I saw it, the muffled clump-clumping of hoofs.

A herd of bison was behind us, coming down the road without slowing. There were at least two dozen of them and they passed within an inch of the bus. These massive-headed, humpbacked, long-haired beasts moving in unison in a lumbering gallop, then sprinting faster.

I could feel the ground shaking. They moved so gracefully and with such freedom that I wanted to run with them to wherever they were going.

Jake Pritchett got out his phone. Later, when he posted his video online it went viral. Survivalists and doomsayers said that the bison were telling us the supervolcano would blow, or that the animals sensed something we couldn't yet know, or that End Times were near and the bison symbolized the Final Battle.

I put my camera up to my eye and snapped some frames.

Watching this blur of dark against light, I questioned whether the extraordinary event was a good sign or an omen of things to come. For me those bison represented the turning point. The moment my heart went all in for Gabriel Finch, and there was no going back.

22

As our bus pulled up to Hawthorn, Nan honked, like I needed help finding the Airstream. When I climbed aboard she
scanned the parking lot for Billy, who we were supposed to
drop off at Affinity. We watched him dive into Martin Goodwin's Camaro. The yellow car sped off.

"Fun trip?" she asked.

"Had a ball," I told her, settling in on the bench by the driver's seat and resting my legs on my bag. I felt exhausted beyond
belief.

"You get some decent shots?" Nan asked.

"A few."

"Your father left money."

"Don't want it."

"I'd take it if I were you. These occasions are rare."

Once home I unpacked, threw a load of laundry into the
machine and went online to check the MoMA site. Reception
was bad in the park and on the ride back, so I hadn't been able
to pay the contest any attention.

I was startled to see how much the mosaic had moved up in
ranking. There were a lot of comments now, along with hundreds of thumbs-up and shares. *Are those really bullets? Who's
the artist? Where's it at? That's mental. That's sick. That's whack.*

The website had received 300,000 visitors and over 100,000 votes had been cast.

I knew it was too early to get my hopes up. But I still wanted to go to the farm right away to give him the good news.

In the kitchen, Nan was at the table updating her obit, modifying a sentence here and there. She did this every few months.

"Where you off to?" she asked as I rushed to put on my boots, grabbing the keys to the truck.

"Farm."

"Blizzard's coming. You shouldn't be driving out there."

I looked out the window. "Sky's blue. It's fine."

"Take your toque and mitts. Put on a warmer coat."

I did what she asked, stole a piece of apple off her plate and left.

Once I got onto the highway the wind picked up, whipping snow across the road. I recalled the shamal wind that Gabriel had described, as I slowed to avoid losing control.

I pulled up at the farm beneath a graying sky and crystallized sun. The barn and the house creaked as I passed by, and I thought how lonely Gabriel must be with no one to talk to but his dog and the crows.

He'd left the blast door open again. It gave me a small thrill, knowing he'd probably done it in case I stopped in. I pulled the door closed before making my way down the ramp.

Inside the silo I found him at the top of the scaffolding platform, pressing shells to the ceiling. He'd aimed the track lights upward to shine on his new scene of sun, crescent moon and stars.

I'd thought the mosaic was done when we submitted it to the contest, but now he was filling the top of the dome, too. When he saw me, he climbed down, jumping from the lowest platform to the ground.

"What happened to getting rid of the ceiling?" I asked. Storm lay on my blanket. The dog raised his head, licked his front paws and went back to sleep.

"This is in case that doesn't pan out. Welcome back," he told me. "Where's whatshisname?"

My stomach clenched. "We split up."

"Is that a fact." He gave me a slow half-smile.

As we walked over to where Storm rested, I noticed that Gabriel was limping again. This probably meant he'd been working nonstop.

"Not to get your hopes up, but your entry's doing well," I told him, trying to mask my excitement. "See for yourself."

He removed his headlamp while I pulled the contest page up. But when I passed him the tablet he gently pushed my hand away.

"Wouldn't want to lose focus," he told me. "Can't have outside noise."

"I don't think you need to worry about outside noises in here," I said. It was so cold we could see our breath.

Gabriel clicked the space heaters on. When he sat back down beside me and offered me his lumberjack I got a feeling like there were fireflies in my chest. I put the shirt on. The long sleeves went past my hands. I brought the cuffs up to my nose and cheeks, pretending to warm my face so I could smell the shirt. The whiff of firepit mixed with tobacco was intoxicating.

"So is this the Mesopotamian sky or the Montana sky?" I asked him, tilting my head back.

He tilted his head back, too, our hands an inch apart.

"There's only one sky, Twyla Lee."

23

We tiled the floor for a few hours before packing up to grab a
bite at the farmhouse. But when we got to the top of the ramp,
the blast door wouldn't budge. We went back down into the
silo and checked the tablet for local news and weather.

A violent blizzard was raging through the region, with
whiteouts, driving winds and drifting snow. Visibility was zero.
Highways were shut down. By closing the blast door and letting
a snowbank accumulate in front of it, I'd barricaded us inside.

"I could've sworn I'd kept it open so this wouldn't happen,"
Gabriel said.

"Yeah. About that ..."

Gabriel turned to Storm. "Sorry, buddy. She's trapped us.
Nothing we can do but wait it out." Then he turned to me.
"Let's keep at 'er."

I phoned Nan.

"Sit tight," she said. "At least you two could survive a typhoon
down in that container. I'll be sure to tell your father. He'll be
real happy about this." Apparently Dad had got into town just
before the storm hit.

We cranked up the space heaters and Gabriel prepared
some MREs.

"What will we do for washrooms?" I finally said.

"Plumbing's fine in the missileer's bathroom."

"But you told Billy —"

"That was to get rid of him," he said in a low voice.

After we ate we carried on with the tiling and did ten more feet of tessellation.

Working next to Gabriel, there was no such thing as time passing. I only stopped when my fingers were too numb to move. It must have been the middle of the night by then.

I even showered in the tiny enclosure, which miraculously had hot water. There were towels draped across a shelf in there, and soap and shampoo. The white bar smelled like almonds and the shampoo like spearmint gum. I stayed in there a long time before wrapping my body in one of his soft musky towels.

I got dressed again and went back to the dome, where Gabriel was putting on some music. Clarinets blasted through the mini speakers. Nan played these types of tunes sometimes, from her own mother's era, and she'd taught me how to dance to them when I was small. The music was from the Roaring Twenties, between the Old Wars.

"We should get our bodies heated up," I told him, flipping my wet hair into a ponytail. I did a fast step, kicking my feet forward and back, moving my palms in circles to the left and right, doing all the flapper moves I could think of.

It was a dance, Nan told me, that was an escape from the horror of war. A dance that said the good times would never end.

I grabbed Gabriel's arms and pulled them forward and back to get him going.

He laughed as he moved around uncomfortably. Then out of nowhere he stepped in closer, took my hand and put it on his shoulder, and placed his other hand in the small of my back.

As we danced, I couldn't feel any shake in his hand.

When the song ended we stood on the spot, until he stepped back and took a bow.

Then the heaters short-circuited and the track lights went out with a pop. The backup power system went on, humming and casting a spooky glow around the space.

We collected all the blankets we could find. Gabriel dragged a mattress over from the control room sleeping quarters. He put a sleeping bag on the mattress, motioned for me to get in and went and sat against the wall across from me.

I opened the sleeping bag and sat up.

"You'll get hypothermia," I said. I could hardly see him through the dim emergency lighting. He looked like a pale blue ghost.

"Come on, Gabriel," I told him, suddenly feeling shy. "I'm freezing."

It was the first time I said his name to him out loud.

He hobbled over like his legs were stiffening, took off his boots and got into the sleeping bag. We called Storm over but the dog stayed near the entryway as if to guard it.

Gabriel pulled the other blankets over us and lay on his back, and I could feel his leg against mine. I followed his gaze up to the top of the dome.

"Know what I missed over there?" he said after a few minutes. "Flannel sheets." I thought he'd go on but he didn't. He just crossed his arms behind his head and closed his eyes.

"You were going to tell me about King Gilgamesh," I said.

He took a deep breath. "Before I enlisted, I wanted to study the Greeks and Romans. The *Iliad* and the *Odyssey* were game changers for me."

"Your mom mentioned that."

"I never knew what came before. Then I end up near the birthplace of Western civilization, between the Tigris and the Euphrates. There we were with our tanks and our guns and our camps and our bombers."

"You said it was your interpreter … who told you about Gilgamesh?"

"He gave me the epic and some printouts on Uruk. In exchange for my Stephen Kings."

"Are you still in touch?"

"No." He paused. "So, back to the story. You want the specs?"

"Sure."

"It's about love. And it's about the dangers of having absolute convictions about what's good and what's evil."

"So, no plot."

"There's a plot."

"Because it seems all philosophical and whatnot."

"Take it easy. I'm getting there."

I rubbed my hands together and blew on my fingers to keep them warm.

"Gilgamesh rules over Uruk but he's a tyrant. So the gods create a wild man named Enkidu to stop him. Gilgamesh and Enkidu fight it out, then become best friends. After that they set out to kill the monster Humbaba, who guards the Cedar Mountain, because Gilgamesh wants to be famous. Later, they also kill the Bull of Heaven. Basically they pull a bunch of stunts to offend the gods. So the gods kill Enkidu as punishment."

"Why just Enkidu?"

"Because the gods decide one of the heroes has to kick it. And they pick Enkidu. We don't know why."

"Why punish them for killing monsters?"

"That's the thing. At first we think Gilgamesh is the hero for slaying the monster. So he's good and the monster's bad, right? But then we find out that the monster Humbaba was ordered by one of the gods to kill Enkidu. Humbaba was only doing his job. So the opposite could be true, too. Who's to say that Gilgamesh isn't evil and the monster good? It's arbitrary, depending on which side you're on."

It was too deep for me.

"So the mosaic's your tribute to King Gilgamesh?" I wished he'd told me all this before I filled out the MoMA application.

"It's not a tribute to anything."

"What about the immortality bit?"

"Gilgamesh loses it after Enkidu dies. He's gutted. So he sets out on a quest to find the secret to eternal life. That's the second half of the epic."

"Does he find it?"

"Nah."

"Then what's the point?"

"He wises up. Figures out that life's fleeting. Eat, drink and be merry 'cause tomorrow we die."

"Is that what's on your arm?"

He raised his bent arm above us.

"This is a passage about a river," he said. "That takes us all away."

"Like the Flood?"

"Something like that."

We looked at each other at the same time. My heart sounded like marching soldiers in my ears.

He opened his mouth like he was going to say something, before he turned away and rubbed his fingers. His hands were covered in cuts from the brass.

Eventually he fell asleep. I could still see his face in the faint backup lighting. Every so often he chomped his teeth down hard. As I traced the scar along his cheek, my finger a millimeter from his skin, it occurred to me that Valentine's Day had just passed.

———

We were in there another full day before Nan, Travis and Dad came with Reg Voigt's plow. While we waited to be rescued, we had time to work on tessellating a good chunk of the ramp, and I was able to document the silo more meticulously than I'd done for the contest entry. I had extra rolls of film in my backpack and I opened the aperture setting, adjusted the shutter speed and used my flash to compensate for the low light. I shot the whole thing, including the new ceiling.

I didn't second-guess my photos anymore, now that the mosaic had gained traction. With black-and-white you could see the tones, texture and depth of the cartridges and casings, the cells forming patterns and pictures like in close-ups of a honeycomb.

It was night when they arrived. Nan texted, and we heard the sound of the machine before the door opened enough for our bodies to pass. We stepped out into the dark and Nan hugged me and Dad watched, probably not sure if he should thank or punch Gabriel.

"Good to see you again." Travis extended a hand to Gabriel as Storm ran through the snow.

It was obvious they wouldn't leave until they got a tour of the silo.

After we all stepped into the dome, Gabriel tried the lights and they were working again.

"Holy mackerel," Travis said.

Nan just stood there shaking her head. She was speechless, which was rare. I thought I saw her chin wobbling until she covered her mouth with her hand and walked around, touching the walls like she couldn't believe what she saw.

"Pretty rad, fella," Dad said, slapping Gabriel on the back.

"Twyla helped a lot," Gabriel replied. "I couldn't have done it without her."

When we got outside again, Travis pointed to the Northern Lights. Everyone turned off their flashlights to watch the palette of greens stroking the sky. You could hear them, too, this strange barely audible crackling.

Hooper told us once that there is no utopia. Utopia literally means no place. And I knew that the last place a utopia could ever exist would be in the land of nuclear missiles.

But as we stood there in the snow, looking up in wonder, it felt like we were part of a utopian landscape. It was magic.

24

Day and night, plows grated through Halo, their oversized blades and underbody scrapers sounding like prehistoric beasts. Within a week the roads and highways were clear and the district reopened schools.

It was hard to go to class. Hard to go to Taco John's and hard to think about anything but Gabriel and the mosaic.

I sent Lucinda regular updates and in exchange she sent photos of alpacas. When I texted Mom, she said she was knee-deep in her new juice business, selling at trade shows and fairs. As for Dad, he'd gone AWOL with the truck.

When I got to Hawthorn the morning it reopened, I was relieved to see that Jeremy's seat was empty. Billy rushed in as the bell went.

We hadn't seen each other since our break-up. As he brushed past my desk and crossed the room, I uttered a meek "Hey," but he didn't look my way. He wore a storebought scarf.

Evidently his plan was to pretend I didn't exist until the school year ended.

"That's gotta hurt," Jolene said from her seat behind mine. "Then again, you did dump him."

When I turned around to face her she was squinting, pressing her fingers to her temples.

"How did the audition go?" I asked.

"Spectacularly. I'm sure I got the part." Her face was bloated, her eyes puffy.

Hooper, on the other hand, was glowing. We all knew she and Dodge had hooked up at Yellowstone. She wore jodhpurs, riding boots and a checked blazer, like she was on her way to the showjumping championships. She was devoting the week to Greek mythology and she was excited.

"You're each getting a myth to share in class. Give me a double-spaced page on your god, goddess, hero or heroine for tomorrow."

The slip of paper that Hooper dropped onto my desk read, *Moirai. Run, spindles, run, and draw the fateful thread.*

"What's yours?" Jolene tapped my shoulder.

"No idea."

"I got Ajax. Like the detergent or the outlet, I guess. Why's so much stuff named after this dude?" she called out to Hooper.

Hooper returned to Jolene's desk and pointed to the sentence below his name. "Your hint's *The great warrior conquered by his own sorrow.* Aren't you the least bit curious, Jo?"

She gave us the rest of class to get started. I looked up Moirai. My gods were the Fates: three sisters who determined every human being's life from birth to death using nothing but a thread. The first sister, Clotho, spun our thread and decided when we were born. Within days of our birth the second sister, Lachesis, measured our thread, locking down how long we'd live, and our destiny. Atropos was the third sister. She decided how we died based on the stuff we did, cutting our thread of life with her scissors. With few exceptions, what these sisters wove couldn't be changed. Even gods had to stoop to their decisions.

After reading up on the Moirai, I visited the contest site. Gabriel's entry had flat-lined. Other works had become more popular than the mosaic. I scrolled through the top contenders, which included a dress made from dust bunnies, landscapes carved into books, a portrait made from cremation ashes, and a three-dimensional painting of sharks that looked so real it was as if they were swimming right at you. There was a sculpture of a naked woman made of bicycle chains, and a labyrinth built from shattered glass.

Each entry was more impressive than the last. Gabriel had stiff competition.

I felt faint. He had to win. It was the only thing that would allow him to focus on his true calling and get over the past: the terrors of the wars, the death of his little sister. Once his work became recognized, anything could happen.

Dad showed up long enough to sleep through a day, then leave again for an extra shift in the patch. He didn't ask about the silo, or about Gabriel. He hadn't asked about Yellowstone, either.

As I watched him drive away with Reg Voigt, I got a text from Jolene.

You see this? it said, with a link. Someone had tweeted about the mosaic.

The Twitter handle was @Hero but the tweets said things like, *He's worse than a deserter. Pro-Raghead freak. Time to court-martial the criminal.*

"Hero" had set up a photo-share page with pictures of the silo, but they weren't the ones on the MoMA site that I'd taken. These pictures included the long dark access tunnel, the eerie control room, the ammo boxes lining the walls and close-ups of the cartridges and casings rather than the images that they formed. There were also pictures of Gabriel working on the scaffolding, wearing his gas mask while he blowtorched the walls.

Someone had been there watching without him knowing. It made his mosaic seem like the work of a madman.

I forced myself to stay calm but the tweets and images went viral fast. By 2 a.m. people were calling him an armed and dangerous nut job.

If I didn't find a way to contain the damage, we were done, all thanks to a few of Halo's narrow-minded cretins. I tweeted the MoMA links and asked people to see what they were seeing from a different perspective.

Once cyberspace made the connection between Hero's posts and the contest entry, everything flipped again. The mosaic started trending, and by 4 a.m. people were calling Gabriel an artist and a Marine who "got it."

The votes were split. Half hated what he'd done, and half thought he was a genius. The vets weighed in, too, and those in active service. Before long someone posted the exact location of the silo.

All day I watched Gabriel's entry shoot up until it reached the top-twenty slot, then the top ten. By the time the voting deadline passed at midnight on March 1st, the mosaic was in ninth place.

I phoned him right away. He always picked up when I called now.

"You made it!" I cried.

"You don't say."

"Oh my God. Don't get too excited."

"You woke me."

"I'm *happy* for you."

"Maybe let's get some sleep. Night."

"Hey, wait, Gabriel."

"Mhmm."

"I'm doing this thing on the Moirai in class. Do you know them?"

"You mean the Fates."

"Yeah."

It sounded like he was sitting up then. He didn't say anything for some time.

"I don't believe in fate," he finally told me. "I used to think our destinies were written out but they're not. And it's way too late to be discussing this."

"I'll see you tomorrow."

"You will."

"Bright and early!"

"Not too bright or too early."

I hardly slept.

I let myself imagine Gabriel winning. He'd be able to keep the farm. We'd give the place a fresh coat of paint. Maybe get a vegetable garden going. I'd help him with his new works of art, and I'd start my own photo projects. I still wanted to try my hand at landscapes. We were in the right location for it. I didn't even want to leave Halo anymore. I felt a pang, thinking about our future.

At 6 a.m. my phone buzzed. The caller ID flashed a New York number that wasn't Mom's.

"Hello?" I said tentatively.

"This is Elizabeth Malone calling from the Museum of Modern Art. Is this the studio line for Gabriel Finch?"

"Uhm … I'm Twyla Lee. I posted his entry. I mean, I helped out. Sort of."

"You're his gallerist?"

"No. I'm … a friend."

"We'd like to view the mosaic." She spoke quickly, like she'd had a lot of coffee already. "We're making arrangements to be there on March twentieth. You're our last stop after Idaho. We'll have a two-hour window."

"Looking forward to it," I said, trying not to sound too excited.

"My assistant will send you the itinerary. Please make sure that Mr. Finch is in attendance. See you soon."

I jumped up and down on my bed, screaming until Nan rushed in.

"MoMA's coming!" I yelled.

"I'll be damned."

"Don't wait on me for dinner," I told her, throwing on my jeans and following her into the kitchen. "I'm going to the farm after class."

We had less than twenty days to perfect the installation. There was the floor to finish, not to mention the clean-up, including removing all the scaffolding and reconfiguring the lighting.

Nan was still in her Slanket. She pursed her lips. "Your parents and I are concerned. That you're growing too attached."

"Don't be a killjoy," I said.

She sighed and shook her head. "Git along," she told me.

I kissed her, grabbed some toast off her plate and was out the door.

25

Jeremy wasn't in class again and neither was Billy, so the day went by without a hitch and I skipped last period to get to the farm early. Like always Gabriel had left the blast door open, and I heard Storm barking from inside. It was colder than usual in the tunnel, and darker. As dark as a shadow's shadow. I found a flashlight and made my way down the ramp.

Gabriel was resting against a wall and drinking a beer. Several more feet of tessellation had been completed, even though most of the lights were off. His eyes were closed and "Brothers in Arms" by Dire Straits was playing.

I flipped the space heaters on before sliding down next to him to listen to the haunting guitar chords and sad lyrics about fields of destruction and wanting to return home to mist-covered mountains and farms.

He flattened his can and opened another. "You remember the game Operation?"

"Sure."

"That's what it's like there."

I didn't know how to fill him in on the news when he was so gloomy.

"Do you have a plan, Twyla?" he asked.

"My plan's to help you win. The judges called and they're coming!"

"But what's your plan beyond the contest?"

"New York City's my plan. And seeing MoMA. And then, if you need a hand on the farm to get it going again, I was thinking —"

"I mean," he interrupted, "what are you going to do with your life."

"I like figuring things out as I go along."

"My plan was to quit football and study ancient economics. But I fouled up."

"You can still get a degree. That's what the GI Bill's for."

"What I'm telling you is, if you know what you want, don't delay it or it won't happen."

"Listen, I know I don't understand what you've been through but I can help with —"

"Do you want to go to college?"

"Not particularly."

"What do you want to do?"

"Take pictures. Probably do weddings and parties, to start."

"You're a photojournalist. I've seen your grandfather's work."

I shook my head. "I don't want to go down that road."

"Maybe you have to." He stood and pulled me up, too. "It was selfish of me to involve you in this. It's a waste of time."

He turned on the floodlights.

As the wall panels lit up, I saw that the entire mosaic had been spray painted, vandalized beyond recognition.

Uruk and its magnificent landscape and people had been overlaid with obscene images of men and women having sex in every imaginable position, with random vulgar words written around them like *cock*, *pussy* and *cunt*. Cans of red paint had been thrown against the dome, dripping to the ground like barrels of blood.

The vandals had climbed the scaffolding and gotten to the scenes higher up, too. They'd sprayed TRAITOR HAJI LOVER in thick black letters over the ceiling's stars, sun and moon.

But the main target was the crouching lovers, who were coated in a brown goo, which I realized was cow shit when I rushed over to the walls and the stench hit me.

The paint was still fresh. As I tried to wipe it off I only spread it around more. I ran to another wall and rubbed at the graffiti with my hands. I grabbed a rag from the ground and tried scrubbing.

Jeremy and his crew must have come during the night.

"We've got to call the cops," I said. "They'll arrest him."

"Who?"

"Jeremy Colt."

"This means game over."

"You can still win," I told him, feeling sick, not believing my own words.

He finished his beer and sat back down. "I don't know if I have the energy."

"You can't let these assholes break you, Gabriel."

He sighed and picked up an aerosol can from the ground.

"Only option would be to spray the whole thing," he said, shaking the can. "Not to mention we'd need a goddamn fire hose for all that dung."

"We have to get it back to how it was."

"You can never go back to how it was, Twyla."

"Just shut up and start scrubbing," I told him.

"When did you say that outfit's coming?" he asked.

"Let's not get stuck on details." I didn't want to tell him that we had under three weeks to get it all cleaned up. In truth, it was impossible. The mosaic was completely destroyed.

As I drove back home I passed a convoy of flatbeds hauling tanks and equipment away, taking Angstrom Air Force Base apart to relocate it. It was really happening. Our town wouldn't exist much longer.

I found Nan at the kitchen table working on a blackout poem. She did these from time to time when she was feeling troubled, which usually meant she was worrying about Dad and Mom, or me, or money.

The logic behind blackout poems was that when you looked at a newspaper article, certain words floated to the surface and stood out. Nan took a marker and crossed out word after word until only a few words remained, which formed the poem.

I pulled my boots off and put my head on the table.

"What's happened?" she asked, setting her marker aside.

"Jeremy totaled the mosaic. I've never known anyone so evil." I looked at her, my eyes welling up. "I told Gabriel we'd clean it before the judges come, but there's no way."

Nan gave a low whistle. "Everyone's talking about this now." She typed something on her laptop and pointed to the screen. "He has tremendous support." She showed me feeds from Marines and citizens against the wars. "These young men and women are expecting to see something."

I sniffed and blew my nose. "I thought you didn't want me hanging around him."

"That's a separate issue."

I scanned her poem. The article was about nuclear warfare:

Take ▮▮ ▮▮ ▮▮▮▮ who's ▮▮▮▮ ▮▮ ▮▮▮▮▮▮ ▮▮ left ▮
▮▮▮▮▮▮▮▮ ▮▮▮▮ to Last Mountain River ▮▮▮▮ ▮▮,
gone ▮ ▮▮▮▮▮▮▮▮▮ ▮▮ ▮▮▮ is ▮ ▮▮▮▮▮▮ this
▮ ▮ ▮▮▮ life here ▮▮▮ ▮ ▮▮▮▮▮▮ ▮▮ ▮▮ ▮ ▮▮.

Last Mountain River was down south, near Fort Stelan. Folktales said that the rugged, cold blue stream had special healing powers.

"Can you phone me in sick tomorrow?" I asked Nan.

"That's what I call taking advantage of a situation." She brought her chin down a fraction and peered at me over her glasses. "Just this once. Don't make me regret it."

I took a hot bath and tried not to think about the hopeless task ahead. Then I put my pajamas on, crawled into bed and went on Twitter to see what new lies were being spread.

But the trend now revolved around the mosaic's ranking. People tweeted about how they were going to make a trip to Halo to see it. How they'd never heard of anything like it. How finally one member of the military was expressing what many others had been feeling for so long.

26

The next morning there was a group gathering on the property, near the barn. Storm barked nonstop as they huddled together against the cold. I pulled up next to the local news truck and a writer from the *Interceptor* who was often at Hawthorn covering Buffalos games. There were also some Triple Ds there, and the vet Gabriel had spoken with on Main Street before Christmas.

"Can we take a peek?" the old man asked.

A Triple D stepped forward. "We have a right. We were there."

"Sorry, but it's not open for viewing yet," I told them. "Check back next month."

"Should we inquire with Fort Stelan? Maybe they can tell us what he's up to. He's one of theirs, right?" the reporter pressed. "Or would Angstrom be the better bet, since it involves a nuke site?"

I'd been worrying about when the military would show up. They'd be afraid an antiwar mosaic would lower morale. Officials were probably already figuring out how to put an end to the project without looking like the bad guys.

I sent the group away and dragged Storm to the house.

Gabriel was drinking coffee and sketching at the kitchen table. I helped myself to a cup as he pulled back a chair for me, without looking up from his drawing.

The sketch was of a low sun above a drift of sand. The sun was enormous, carrying the weight of daylight away with it as two black choppers flew across its face.

"I read this article by NASA that says the sun's going dark," he told me.

"Why?"

"Holes in the solar surface."

"Do you think the world will end?"

"Eventually."

"Does it scare you?"

"I try not to think about it."

We got solvents from the barn, loaded up the wagon and walked through the snow-covered field. We locked the blast door from inside, then rolled our gear down the ramp and into the dome.

Gabriel turned on the lights and my heart lurched when I saw the ruined masterpiece again. Mostly it was the bottom half of the mosaic that was defaced.

We started with the worst, and I gagged as I wiped the shit off the wall and dumped buckets of soapy water, Lysol and vinegar over the lovers. We had to use toothbrushes and Q-tips to get at what had seeped between the cartridges and casings.

When we were done we threw everything into garbage bags, and I fished for the small bottle of vanilla body mist I kept in my backpack, spraying the scene over and over again.

"It's psychological," I told Gabriel.

After that we soaked rags in stinking solvents. Gabriel climbed the scaffolding to the top of the dome and I worked on the lower scenes. The paint came off the surfaces, but again it was harder to get at the cracks between the ammo.

I worked until my muscles ached, and even then we'd only managed to clean about ten square feet between the both of us. And an alarming number of cartridges and casings had come loose. The solvents were reacting with the glue, causing the metals to detach from the wall as we scrubbed.

Finally Gabriel climbed down and threw off his gloves and I did the same.

I lay on my back and listened. The ammo fell like raindrops, chiming around us. I watched Gabriel lie down, too, and thought about the months he'd spent alone in the silo. During those hours, did he replay the wars in his mind? Was he thinking about the other paths he could have taken? I couldn't bring myself to ask him these questions.

I sat up and reached for a mask and handed one to him.

"Let's go," I said.

"There's no point," he told me.

"I'm not flunking my volunteer credits because of you. I've got to identify results, and this mess isn't fit for identifying."

"Your service obligations were for housework. You've flunked already."

"My contract stipulates that my service hours are for helping you out with whatever needs doing."

"Anyone ever tell you you're a nuisance?"

"My Nan. Regularly."

We got up again and worked on a panel side by side. As I scrubbed, Gabriel said, "Top three foods."

"Pardon?"

"What are your favorite foods?"

"Uhhh. Anything but Mexican."

"Don't be indecisive. Name three."

"Okay. Wild strawberries. Dad's barbecued ribs. And poutine."

"Poutine?"

"A Canadian dish of Nan's. Gravy on cheese on fries. And I suppose yours would be MREs, MREs and MREs?"

"Swiss mushroom burger, high plains chili, huckleberry pie."

"Top three chores," I said.

"Chores? You don't have the swing of this game."

"Just go."

"Vacuuming."

"Lame."

"It relaxes me. Same for cleaning windows and washing dishes."

"You wouldn't know it from the sink in your kitchen."

"Funny. And yours would be?"

"Helping Nan with the Airstream."

"That's not a chore."

"Putting away groceries."

"I guess that qualifies."

"Laundry when we have the nice-smelling fabric softener. And feeding the pets."

"You have no pets."

"But if we did, that would be one of my favorite chores."

"Top three things you love about Halo."

"Really?" I sighed. "Maybe the summer rodeo. The view from Hill 5. And the What the Hay Bale Trail. Your go."

"Our cowboy poets."

"But they're awful!"

"They're so bad they're good. Next up's fly-fishing. And our sky. And the rough roads that lead to wondrous places."

"That's four."

"Forget sky, then. Sky's a given."

"Top three things you hate about Halo," I said.

"You're really not getting this. Okay. Ajax Outlets. The smell coming from Sunnyside on windy days. And Angstrom."

"My turn. I hate our nukes and silos. Aside from yours, I mean."

"Fair enough."

"And I wish Tomahawk would burn to the ground. And Jeremy Colt."

"Spoken with true passion. I don't think a person qualifies."

"It does in my version of this game."

"Moving right along then. Top three places you want to visit, other than New York."

I scrubbed as I thought, but came up blank. Aside from California, I hadn't thought about it.

"Come on," Gabriel said. "Everyone has a top-three travel list. Mine are Crete. Paris. And Graceland. And yours would be ..."

"London," I finally said. "To see Buckingham Palace. And the buses."

"That's original."

"And Graceland is?"

"Point taken."

"Two, Paris."

"You're copying."

"Who doesn't want to see Paris?"

"True. And three?"

"Uruk."

Gabriel stopped scrubbing. "You can't go there."

"So what."

"So pick somewhere else."

"This is your stupid game, not mine."

He put a hand on my shoulder. "Let's call it a night. Your gran'll run me over if you don't get home."

I checked my phone. It was past eleven.

We walked into the middle of the space to assess our work. We'd made a little progress, but not much. Gabriel looked up at the defaced ceiling, deep in thought.

"Twilight," he finally said. "Like that final color in a rainbow."

27

The next morning when I went into the kitchen, Dad was sitting there with Nan, back from another shift, the both of them waiting for me.

"Eat something," Nan said, gesturing to the plate of hash browns on the table.

"You're pale," Dad added.

"Not hungry," I told them, pouring a coffee. I had a splitting headache from the solvent fumes.

"This arrived for you yesterday." Nan handed me an envelope from Berkeley, which I put into my backpack.

"You're not going to open it?" Nan said. "What if you got in?"

"Fat chance. I have to miss class again today. Actually, probably all week." Nan gave me the stink-eye. "It won't make a difference to my grades," I added. "Just tell the attendance office I have the flu."

"Absolutely not."

I sat down and took her hand as Dad sat back, crossing his arms.

"This is the most important thing I'll ever do in my life," I told her.

"I doubt that very much."

"His future depends on this. I have to help, especially now that everyone wants to see it. You said so yourself yesterday."

"Restore it outside of school hours."

"There's no time. We've got to put in full days."

Nan clucked her tongue. "When this is finished I'm locking you in your room until you're caught up and ready for finals," she said. Dad watched me without a word. "I hope you know what you're doing, Granddaughter," she added.

Dad let me take the truck. On my way out of town I pulled over at Viewpoint Boulevard. The fields were thawing out, glistening in the stark pre-spring light. I texted Gabriel that I was on my way. Then I phoned Travis. When I told him about the vandalism he sounded upset. He said he'd get my shifts covered for the week and not to worry.

There wasn't anyone waiting on the property this time. Maybe because it was still early, or maybe everyone had lost interest already. Regardless, Gabriel had tied Storm to a boulder near the blast door, so he could warn us of trespassers. The dog licked my hand as I passed through into the silo, where Gabriel was already working.

"Took you long enough," he said, tossing an apple my way.

"Health kick?" I asked. "You're not going to make me jog the field, I hope."

"That's tomorrow."

I walked around the space. Overnight more cartridges and casings had fallen from the walls. The solvents were still reacting to the glue. But this time I'd brought my photos with me. I laid them out on the ground like a map to determine which type of ammo went where. Meanwhile, Gabriel replaced each bit of metal in a pattern he knew by heart, bringing the tiger's face back, the palm trees, the rivers and the desert.

A few hours later when we were finally making headway,

we heard Storm barking, and echoes of voices traveling down the ramp.

Gabriel reached for the blowtorch and I grabbed my phone preparing to call 911, when Trav and Carm appeared at the door in coveralls.

"Ay, Dios mío," Carm mumbled, looking around.

"We thought you could use some help," Travis said.

Gabriel pulled the gas mask up onto his forehead.

"Actually, we could. Don't take it personally, Twilight."

My pulse sped up when I heard my new nickname.

Carm licked a finger and rubbed at some paint.

"Gimme access to the house," she told us. "I'll make a kitchen mix to take off the graffiti. Mexico City trick."

Gabriel pulled the keys from his pocket and gestured for her to follow him. He was locking the farmhouse now. I set Travis up with the zoo scene, handing him a toothbrush and a box of Q-tips.

"They really look alive, don't they," he said, admiring the animals before he got to work.

I set up nearby, and Travis hummed as we scrubbed.

"You love him, hey," he said after a while.

"Jesus, Trav."

"Just sayin'."

"What leads you to this conclusion?"

"Christmas luncheon."

I felt myself blush and turned away.

"The judges are coming soon," I told him.

He looked around at the mess. "There's no shame in it, Twills," he said. "Take me 'n' Carm. Anything's possible."

Carm came back with a bucket of sloppy water that smelled like lime and Tabasco sauce. She rubbed at a wall with her rag. The girl had more elbow grease than all of us combined.

We watched as the paint came off and the metals themselves changed into oily reflections like fish skin.

Travis turned to me. "See? It'll be done in a jiff. Let's divvy this potion up and get going."

Like clockwork Trav and Carm came back every day after their shifts during the first of the two and a half weeks we had left to restore the mosaic. By the end of that first week Nan and Dad showed up, too. When they arrived, Nan surveyed Gabriel on his scaffolding, where he was restoring the ceiling, and Trav and Carm hard at work on the ground. Half the mosaic was still covered in graffiti, but the half we'd been scrubbing was looking better than it did before. Carm's concoction made it so shiny that we could see our own faces in the cartridges and casings.

"Put us to work," Nan said.

It was the first time I'd seen Dad without a beer in his hand in ages. By the end of the night, he'd gotten through a whole panel, completely restoring the orchard.

Nan followed my photos and put the fallen ammo in place on the parachute cloth. Then I glued the pieces back onto the wall. We went through dozens of toothbrushes and boxes of Q-tips. We also finished the tiling. There wasn't an inch of visible concrete left once we were done.

On Sunday night we took a break to have a proper dinner in the dome, with real food Nan had brought from Michelle's Diner: chicken and ribs, coleslaw and potato salad.

We were gorging ourselves when we heard boots marching down the ramp in an unbroken rhythm.

A half-dozen armed and uniformed security forces specialists stood in the doorway.

"Which one of you is Gabriel Finch?" the lead guard asked.

"That's me." Gabriel took his time standing up.

None of the men's heads moved as their eyes conducted a recon. Their expressions didn't even change as they scanned the mural.

"This is United States Armed Forces property," the guard barked.

"It's my farm."

"Angstrom has no record that you purchased the silo when it was decommissioned. Your activities are illegal."

Everyone had stopped eating and talking except Nan, who continued gnawing on her drumstick.

"You can take over when I'm done," Gabriel told them.

"We need you to come with us."

Two men stepped forward on either side of him.

My palms started sweating. I stood and approached the lead guard and his squad.

"Excuse me," I said. "So you know, he's got a following."

His eyes narrowed on me.

My mouth felt pasty but I kept going. "It would be a shame if the hundreds of thousands of men and women currently serving, along with the vets and the American citizens who voted for this work of art to represent Halo in a world-class competition, were told that Angstrom shut it down."

"Didn't you say a lot of troops are on their way over to show support?" Dad asked me.

I nodded. "By the good graces of Angstrom."

The guard rubbed his jaw.

"You wouldn't believe how much media attention this thing's getting," Nan said. "Would you like some fried chicken?"

He pulled a pen and notepad from a pocket. "Who did you say you were?"

"Twyla Jane Lee. I've been fortunate enough to participate in this project thanks to your Help a Vet program." I pointed to some dunes. "Look," I told him. "Can you see yourself there? You have to get closer."

He nodded to his men and a few of them approached the mural and touched it.

They took Gabriel away anyhow.

I followed Nan and Dad home and pulled over at Viewpoint to tweet. *Gabriel Finch, creator of the Halo Mosaic, in meetings with Angstrom Air Force Base. Possible new projects ahead?* And *Finch and Angstrom: mysterious meeting. Collaborations for armed forces–commissioned art?*

I messaged MoMA to confirm the details of their visit and I cc'd Angstrom and Fort Stelan. Elizabeth Malone's admin assistant replied and cc'd everyone back, thanking us all for being so accommodating and saying how excited the judges were to view Gabriel's installation. Then I called the reporters from the *Interceptor* and the local TV station to offer them a tour.

Within a few hours Gabriel texted to say that he'd been released from questioning. Soon after, the Forces issued their own statement: *While the United States Armed Forces is in no way associated with this project, we encourage our troops to express themselves through creative means.*

The post received thousands of thumbs-up within minutes.

28

When I went back to school after a week's absence, no one spoke to me aside from Jolene. Even Jeremy, who came into class right behind me, completely ignored me after giving his jock friends some fist bumps.

"I know you did this," I hissed as we sat down.

"No clue what you're talking about."

"Ever heard of karma, Jeremy?"

"He tell you yet?"

"Tell me what?"

"'Bout those he smoked."

"Save your shit-slinging lies," I told him. Then I turned to the rest of the class. "Sergeant Colt wears diapers." I said it loud enough for everyone to hear and then I looked him straight in his ugly face.

Jeremy didn't react but his neck went blotchy.

"Shame on you, Twyla," Jolene said under her breath as Hooper pranced in. "You don't know how hard he's had it with his old man."

I whipped back to face her. "He vandalized the mosaic, Jo. He should be in jail." I felt the rage rising like acid in my throat.

"No, he did not. And I heard you fixed it up again. We all heard you fixed it up real nice. So what's the issue?" She looked off, her hair flat and her makeup runny. It also seemed like she'd put on weight.

Hooper had moved on from mythology to Shakespeare, but she made me talk about the Fates since I'd missed the day when everyone had to discuss their gods and demi-gods.

"What do you think about those Moirai, Twyla?"

"I think sometimes the short thread falls to the wrong person." I glared at Jeremy.

Then out of habit I glanced across the room at Billy. He was watching me and I raised my hand in a low wave. But a vicious look crossed his face like I'd never seen before, so I turned away quickly. I knew he'd been hanging around Jeremy lately. I'd seen them smoking out in the parking lot and driving around in Billy's Jeep.

After passing out a written assignment, Hooper came over to my desk and motioned that I follow her outside.

"What's going on at that farm?" she asked once we were in the hallway, putting her hands on her leather-clad hips and tapping a pointed toe.

"Nothing," I replied.

"I've heard all about the mural and there's gossip about you and Gabe Finch. You're not going there unaccompanied, are you?"

"No."

"Because I could get in serious trouble if that was the case." I laughed involuntarily.

"This is no joke. Don't you give a hoot about your future? You're behind on everything. This isn't the time to be slacking. Your admission to any college depends on these final grades."

"Okay then."

"As for your Help a Vet hours, I suspect those are long done. I'm not an imbecile, Twyla Jane Lee."

I looked down at my boots. "It's none of your business."

"Yes, it is. This scenario is inappropriate. But I'm not reporting it because I get it."

"I doubt that."

"You're bored with your life." She gave me a sad smile. I started to reply but she put her hand up and stopped me. "I've heard enough."

She waited for me to follow her back into the classroom, but I told her that I needed to use the washroom.

I walked over to the trophy cases. I thought that seeing Gabriel in his state championship shots would calm my nerves. But instead of feeling better, a gnawing pain rose in my gut.

Gabriel had texted that he had an appointment at the end of the day, so we couldn't meet until the following morning to carry on with our cleanup. He wouldn't let me work in the dome alone in case the vandals broke in again.

I wondered if he was being vague because it was medical. A couple of days before, when Carm and I were taking a break at the farmhouse, I'd gone upstairs to use the bathroom and had noticed new prescription containers, for arthritis and insomnia.

I only went back to class to grab my bag when the bell rang. I managed to avoid Hooper for the rest of the day, went home and locked myself in my room.

Then Jolene showed up uninvited after her shift at Sunnyside. Nan let her in. She kept biting her lip and started crying when she came into my room and sat on the bed.

"Jeremy was pissed at work today. He locked some freshman in cold storage where they keep the innards. He got fired. You sure put him on a warpath, Twyla."

"Do you get what he did, Jolene?"

"You've got no proof."

"Don't you have dance moves to practice or something?" I asked, wanting her to leave.

"I didn't go to the audition in LA. Mom's not talking to me since I backed out. I'm pregnant." When she got up to get her phone from her purse, she left orange smears on my bedspread. Even though it was still cold outside she was in a miniskirt and had just gotten a spray tan.

"Have you considered —"

"No. No, I won't consider it." She picked at the lint on her top. "I hear they'll be reinstating the draft. That's my baby boy's future."

"How do you know it's a boy?"

"Jer says so." She wiped her tears away and rubbed at the spray-tan stains. "Sorry about the duvet."

Gabriel and I finished the restoration together, just him and me. The judges would arrive in a little over week, and there was only one scene left to repair: the crouching lovers. We'd cleaned them, but they'd been damaged worse than the rest of the mosaic. Under the manure there had also been paint spray. Enough to make it look as though gunfire had spattered them.

The paint had hardened on their bodies and faces the longest. I scrubbed and scrubbed, switching from Carm's solution to the heavy-duty agents. The ammo came loose and started falling to the ground again.

"Ease up, Lady Macbeth," Gabriel finally told me. "The red's hardly noticeable."

"But it's there."

He stepped away from the bride and groom, dropping his bristle brush.

"Thanks for the other day," he said.

"What did they want with you?" I asked.

"To go over the details of my service. That's all." He took his headlamp off and did a quick look around. "I think we're done. Let's light it up."

I stood as Gabriel angled the tripods into their circular formation again.

The mosaic shone. It had a radiance that hadn't been there before. The range of tones and the patterns were more brilliant than ever, and the scenes seemed to move almost fluidly, one into the other.

I was suddenly sad that our work was finished.

"Get up there," he told me, gesturing to the scaffolding.

Slowly and carefully I made my way up the platforms. I put my hands on the flocks of birds, the sand dunes and the golden city. Then I reached the top of the dome and touched the moon and the sun and the stars.

I waved at Gabriel, who looked like a small statue below. Everything was different from high up. Like when you climbed a tree and the world you saw wasn't the one you thought you knew.

When I came back down and jumped from the last platform to the ground like Gabriel always did, I reached out for his hand. I knew we both felt something then, before he pulled back to put supplies away.

I knelt next to him and helped box up the tools.

"Tell me more about Uruk," I finally said.

"Gilgamesh becomes a fair ruler. The end."

I looked at the script on his forearm again. "What about that secret to eternal life?"

"The secret is that there's no secret."

"That's it?"

"After Enkidu dies, Gilgamesh heads out through the wilderness to find his ancestor, Utnapishtim. He's the only one who can help Gilgamesh become immortal. He challenges Gilgamesh to stay awake for six days and seven nights, but Gilgamesh messes it up. As a consolation prize, Utnapishtim tells him where to find a plant that'll take away his fear of death. Gilgamesh finds the plant but a snake eats it."

"After all that? He just dies?"

"Not straight away. He goes back to Uruk changed. He gains wisdom. Accepts his mortality 'cause he knows his people and his city will live on."

"So he thought humankind would live forever?"

"The snake turned him into an optimist."

"And what do you think?"

"I think these silos will outlive us."

"These silos will be our ancient cities, then."

"I suspect so, Twilight."

29

I took it as a good sign that the judges were arriving on the Saturday that happened to be the first day of spring. I got up extra early, polished my boots, braided my hair and even put a little makeup on.

On the flip side, I tried not to take it as a bad sign that this was also the day that Angstrom conducted one final test before it relocated. The test was in conjunction with the country's new emergency-warning system, Alarm Ready, designed to deliver immediate alerts in cases of imminent danger from natural disasters, biohazards, terrorist attacks and other life-threatening events. Between 6 a.m. and 6 p.m., on the hour, the base's speakers would emit a steady high-pitched hum that could be heard throughout Halo and beyond.

Although it was still cold outside, I drove with the window down. Through the melting snow came the wet and earthy smells of thawing ground. Soon buttercups would emerge from the dead grasses, and the creeks and rivers would flow again. Soon I'd graduate and be free to get on with my life. I anticipated the year to come, after Gabriel won the contest and we spruced up the farm and got going on new projects together.

There was a crowd at the farm gate when I got there. Everyone wanted to see the mosaic, and Gabriel had agreed to start letting people through after the judges left. Even Mayor Tubman and his posse were scheduled for a special viewing. In case things got out of order, I'd asked Carm to enlist her cousins, Carlos and Hector, who'd just moved to Halo, as guards. They'd rebuilt the gate and added bolts to it. I waved at them as they opened it to let me through.

In the farmhouse I found Gabriel upstairs adjusting his tie in a mirror. He wore a suit and he was clean-shaven. He'd even gotten a haircut.

"You look so … different without all that hair," I told him.

"Like another person, right?"

"New suit?"

"Trav and Carm strong-armed me to Ajax Outlets. I let them pick it out."

"I like it."

He pulled at his collar. "Don't get used to it," he said.

Alarm Ready sounded.

"Angstrom's testing our new cross-country siren," I explained.

"So I've been told. And here I thought my tinnitus was getting worse." Without the stubbly beard, he was more handsome than ever. He also looked a lot younger.

"By the way, I'll bring Storm back tonight," I told him. I'd dropped the dog off at Travis's the day before to keep him out of the way.

"He's better off with Travis," Gabriel replied. He had a faraway look in his eyes. He thought he was going to lose the farm.

"That's low, giving up your dog already," I said. "Have some faith."

"Alrighty." He ran his hand down my braid and tucked a strand behind my ear, like it was the most natural thing for him to do in the world. "Thank you," he told me. "For helping me finish this."

I hoped we'd kiss then. But it wasn't the time, and I could tell he was getting tense.

"Ready?" I asked.

"Yes, ma'am."

The moment we stepped onto the porch, reporters called out to Gabriel from the gate. We went over to wait for the committee.

Trav and Carm had shown up to help oversee things with Carlos and Hector. In the crowd there were too many Triple Ds to count, and the old vet from Main Street and his cronies, too. I also spotted Hooper and Dodge, and Jolene and Jackie.

"Do you believe in the wars?" a reporter called out, holding her phone toward Gabriel.

"Doesn't matter what I believe," he told her.

"Did your actions cause civilian deaths?" another reporter asked.

"Don't answer that," a vet yelled.

"Do you believe in God?" came a new voice from the crowd, and then another. "Do you consider yourself an honorable Marine?"

Gabriel stepped back, cupping a hand over his ear. "Thanks for coming, everyone," he told them as he moved away from the gate.

I followed him to the house again, where he sat on the porch steps and rubbed his face.

"It's going to be a long day," he said, trying to loosen his collar again.

At exactly 10 a.m. a black sedan with tinted windows from a Shady Springs limo company pulled up, and the crowd parted. We stood as the vehicle stopped in front of us. Then the judges emerged one by one: the curator Elizabeth Malone, the artist known as Renny and the art critic Zohar Berkowitz.

I pushed Gabriel forward, and we introduced ourselves and shook their hands.

Elizabeth Malone had milky skin, red lips and strawberry-blonde hair that shimmered in the sun. She repositioned her large sunglasses on her head and zipped up her expensive-looking leather coat.

"Man. It's freezing. Mind if I document you guys in your environment?"

She stepped back, held up her tablet and tapped it as we stood before the farmhouse.

"À la American Gothic." She smiled.

"We just had breakfast at the Sip 'n Sea," Renny said. "Too bad we missed the mermaids. When do they come on?" He had a full head of gray hair and was dressed like a skater in his hoodie, high-tops and green jeans.

The third judge, Zohar Berkowitz, had the face of a bulldog and wore a wooly sweater. He stretched his short arms in the air and yawned.

As we all walked through the field, Elizabeth Malone caught up to me, struggling along the path in her wedge heels.

"So let's start from the start," she spoke into her tablet, then extended it to me like a microphone. "Halo and its surroundings are embedded with nuclear missile facilities, some with warheads and some empty?"

"That's right." I didn't unnerve her with details.

Ahead of us, Renny scanned the countryside like he was on the lookout for snipers. Zohar Berkowitz trudged behind him, smoking and talking on his phone.

We arrived at the blast door and Gabriel led the group down the ramp.

"Whoa," Elizabeth said quietly as we passed through the control room.

"Never gave World War III much thought till now," Renny said, while Zohar put his glasses on to study the buttons and switches.

In the dome, Gabriel left the judges in extreme darkness at first. Then he turned on the lights, which made a *whoosh, whoosh, whoosh* sound, illuminating the mosaic.

I had to swallow back the emotion welling up in me. I'd concealed sachets of lavender here and there to disguise the chemical smells, and it had worked. A piney floral scent filled the space.

"Phenomenal," Elizabeth spoke to the air.

"Hot damn," said Renny.

"Perspectives are off," said Zohar as he went up to the ammo and sniffed it.

Then they launched some forms on their tablets and took turns asking questions. Elizabeth went first.

"What did you do in the wars?"

"Marine Corps."

"Are you seeking forgiveness through this project?"

"I know that's not possible."

"Excuse me," I stepped between them. "Can you stick to questions about the installation?"

"It's okay, Twyla," Gabriel said, his voice calm.

Elizabeth went on. "One piece for each documented civilian casualty?"

Gabriel looked at her, baffled. "How did you know?" he asked.

"You're not our first war artist." She jotted something down. "You've kept count?"

"This only represents the region where I was stationed."

"And that pile there," Zohar pointed to a pyramid of casings that Gabriel had left in the heart of the dome. "Are those the American dead?"

"Yessir."

I grabbed Gabriel by the sleeve and pulled him aside.

"Why didn't you tell me? I would've included it on your entry form."

"Didn't want to bore you with details."

Elizabeth placed her hands on the wall, running them up it. Then she walked the circle, looking in close and stepping back. She even lay down on the tiled ground. She also went to the ramp area and looked at the installation from there.

"I've seen a lot of mosaics," she said. "But nothing ever like this."

"Naïve art," Zohar said, assessing the scenes. "Folksy."

"Awestriking," Renny said, and shuddered. "Is that a word? Awestriking?" He punched it into his tablet.

"So this is Uruk," Elizabeth continued, looking up at the wall surrounding the palace. She'd really done her research.

"With traces of Baghdad," Gabriel replied, glancing at the zoo animals, then at the lovers crouching against the wall.

"What's CBRN?" Zohar asked.

"Chemical, biological, radiological and nuclear."

"And brain bucket?"

"A helmet."

"Our decision is partly informed by your motivation." Elizabeth spoke gently as she approached Gabriel. "Would you like to add anything in terms of *why* you felt the need to create this?"

Gabriel didn't reply.

She tilted her head, looking into his eyes.

Gabriel studied the crouching lovers again before looking back at Elizabeth.

"I messed up," he finally told her.

Zohar nodded. "Care to elaborate?"

"I can't discuss the details."

In all of fifteen minutes, he'd told the judges more than he'd ever told me. I looked to him for an explanation. But when I saw how his face had drained of color, I kept my disappointment in check.

"Tell them how you're going to blow the lid off," I suggested.

"I want to open up the ceiling," he said, "so natural light streams in."

Everyone followed his gaze upward.

"No way," Elizabeth shook her head, her hair swaying. "You should keep the darkness inside."

She pulled a tin of mints from her pocket and offered them around. Then she checked the time and told us they had to leave.

"We've got enough to go on." She pressed a hand on Gabriel's sleeve.

They wanted a picture. Not of the mosaic, but of the three of them in the launch control room. Zohar made his fingers into the shape of a gun and pointed his hand at Renny, who acted like he was being forced to turn an invisible key, while Elizabeth put a hand to her mouth in pretend horror.

When we led them back up the ramp and outside, Alarm Ready was sounding again.

"What's that awful racket?" Elizabeth asked.

"They're testing over at the base," I told her. "In case of a terrorist attack or some other catastrophe."

"Time to clear out," Renny said.

Elizabeth glanced at the bullet tree.

"Is that part of the installation?" She put a hand on her forehead against the sun to get a better look.

"That's just target practice," Gabriel told her.

"No kidding ..." Her voice trailed off. Then she gave us a big smile. "Well, thanks, guys. Be sure to tune in to the results, okay?"

We were their last stop. The finalists would be posted online in two weeks, on a Friday at 6 p.m. Eastern.

We all shook hands, and the judges got into their black car and drove away, past the crowd at the gate.

We still had fifteen minutes before Carm's cousins would open the site for public viewings. We went back to the house.

"What a disaster," Gabriel said, loosening his tie.

"I think they liked it," I told him.

He pulled something from a shelf and handed it to me.

"I meant to give this to you earlier," he said.

The book was titled simply, *Gilgamesh*. A gold, royal-looking head looked up at me against a sea-blue background.

We were interrupted by a knock on the door. The media was ready to film and talk and document.

Carlos and Hector blocked them and nodded to Gabriel through the screen door that it was time for him to lead everyone to the silo for the first tour. Gabriel raised his chin a fraction and put his jacket on again.

The second he stepped outside everyone swarmed him.

He looked back at me and made a motion with his hand for me to call him later. I wouldn't get a minute of his attention. I figured I might as well split.

30

Waiting for the shortlist announcement was agonizing. At Nan's insistence I focused on classes and caught up on homework. I also picked up some shifts at Taco John's.

After what Gabriel had told the judges about messing up, I kept thinking about the vandalism and Jeremy's accusations. But I knew I had to trust he'd talk about it when he was ready.

When I did stop in at the farm, we couldn't hang around the silo anymore. There was always a tour group inside, being led around by Trav or Carm. People came in droves. I missed the time Gabriel and I had alone in there, but then I reminded myself that his art needed to be shared.

Finally announcement day came. At last bell I ran out of Hawthorn to the truck. I saw Billy eyeing me from the parking lot, leaning against his Jeep. I didn't bother waving.

I picked up some popcorn, licorice and sodas from the Exxon and sped to the farm. Travis had put a sign on the gate that said, *Tours Resume Tomorrow*.

In the farmhouse, Gabriel was on the floor reading. I moved his books off the coffee table and set up the tablet and our snacks while he barely looked up.

He only turned my way after I gave his leg a kick.

"Quit acting like you don't care," I told him.

"Don't want to jinx it," he said.

I refreshed the tablet for fifteen minutes until the stroke of four o'clock when the results were to be made public.

Suddenly the site appeared revamped before us, featuring the works of the three finalists on its homepage, including remarks from the judges. Open commenting was closed, and the forum had been removed.

I scrolled down the page, past Finalist Number 1, the sharks, called *Bottom-dwelling cartilaginous pain and slits in my head because of you, Jeanette* and Finalist Number 2, the glass labyrinth, called *Midlife*, to Finalist Number 3.

The mosaic was the third featured work of art at the bottom of the page. *A moving and significant interpretation of the wars*, was Elizabeth Malone's quote. *A profound, nihilistic portrayal like none other*, said Renny. Zohar Berkowitz's citation simply read, *Ghastly, sublime and absolute*.

The winner would be announced on May 1st, at a ceremony at the Museum of Modern Art in New York City.

I jumped and the bowl of popcorn in my lap went flying.

"Yahoo!" I cried.

Gabriel covered his ears.

"Show some excitement!" I pushed him into the couch. "You did it!"

He shook his head like he couldn't believe it. I made him give me a high five. Then Lucinda was calling. I handed him the tablet and checked my phone as it started buzzing, and caller IDs popped up one by one. *Halo Interceptor*, KYXL News, *Shady Springs Chronicle* and *Pendletown Account*. There was also a message from Elizabeth Malone: *Congrats! See you soon!*

And then, a one-worder from Nan: *Sonofagun*.

Gabriel hung up with his mom.

"I'd advise you to start talking to your fans." I sat down again, out of breath. "Holy toledo," I said.

"It's nice to see you so psyched over this."

"It's a *big* deal!" My phone started up again. "You sure you don't want to take interviews? It'll help the cause."

He furrowed his brow. "I'm sure. And, Twyla."

"Mhmm?" I scrolled and added the new callers to my contacts.

"There's no cause."

I looked up from my phone. "You can stand up for what you believe in now. Everyone's backing you."

"I don't know what I believe in."

"Not war."

"Not war." He shifted uncomfortably on the couch. "I didn't think it would become this ... public."

"Get used to it."

"The thing is ... I don't need to attend some fancy gala."

"You have to represent yourself."

"You can represent me." He slapped my knee like the subject was closed for discussion.

"We said we'd go together," I told him.

"We did?"

"Yes. We did. Besides, MoMA's covering your ticket and mine. As your 'agent.'" I made quotation marks in the air.

He leaned forward and pressed his fingers together to form a steeple.

"Okay," he finally said. "If you want to see New York, we'll go."

31

I accidentally slept in the next morning. Nan swung my bedroom door open and leaned against the doorframe with her coffee.

"Why didn't you wake me up?" I asked as I rushed to get dressed. It was already eleven o'clock.

"It's Saturday. You said you weren't working this weekend, and you were dead to the world. Figured you needed the rest." She trailed after me into the kitchen, and when I grabbed the keys to the truck, she added, "You're not going anywhere, Twinks. Ice storm."

I followed her gaze out the window to where an imperceptible drizzle was falling and freezing over, glazing everything: the Airstream, the driveway and the cars parked along the road, the power lines, fences, trees and houses.

Gabriel didn't respond to my messages. I assumed he wasn't in the farmhouse, so I called his cell but he didn't pick that up, either.

I paced around as the ice rain kept falling.

"Quit that, you're making me nervous," Nan said as she pulled some muffins from the oven. She'd baked them too long and they were dry, but we sat at the table and ate them anyway. Then she switched on the countertop TV and turned to the local news. After the weather special, which said that the town would shut down for the day, maybe longer, a day-old story aired. I recognized a reporter who'd been at the farm.

"Mr. Finch declined to comment on his project," she said. "But one thing's for sure, Halo is proud that the Modern Art Museum has included his mosaic as one of the top contenders in their prestigious competition."

"It's the Museum of Modern Art. Not the Modern Art Museum."

"Don't be stuck up," Nan tsked me.

The anchor moved on to a story about End Times, taking call-ins and discussing how to execute bug-out evacuations and surprise drills, how to live in shipping containers, how to collect seeds for radiation-free food and make antibiotics out of fish food.

Nan switched the TV off and watched me.

"You open that admission letter?"

"Not yet."

"Now's as good a time as any, wouldn't you say?"

I retrieved the envelope from my backpack, tore it open and scanned the contents. I'd been admitted to UC Berkeley's Department of Art Practice based on the photo portfolio I'd submitted with my application.

I handed the letter to Nan.

"I'm not going. It's not like we have the money anyway."

"Would you at least request a deferral instead of flat out declining?"

"I don't want to leave Halo anymore."

"Don't be ridiculous."

"I can do plenty here. You'll be on the road soon and Dad's hardly home. I'll take care of the house while you're both gone."

Nan gave me a sharp look.

"What's the problem?" I asked.

"Problem is you've got a screw loose. There won't be a house or a town for you to care for, in case you've forgotten."

"The houses aren't going anywhere."

"You won't have power or water. You gonna pioneer it?"

"I'll go to Gabriel's. The farms will still be running."

"I can see why you're drawn to him," she said, not taking her eyes off me. "But don't be a fool."

"Like you were a fool with Gramps?"

"No sense in you carrying on the family tradition," she said. "Being with someone who's been around war for too long is like using the same big chopping knife day after day. One day it's gonna cut you deep."

"Over and out," I told her and left the kitchen.

Later on I tried calling and texting Gabriel again, without luck. I figured he was working in the silo, since I knew there were still elements that he wanted to fine-tune. I tried to distract myself with homework. I even vacuumed. And in the evening when he didn't pick up again, I phoned Mom.

"I saw the coverage," she said. "I'm impressed and a little jealous. Your dad tells me you're stuck on this boy."

"You talked to Dad?"

"We've been talking."

"Like, regularly?"

She didn't respond. "You open that Berkeley envelope yet?"

"I got in. But I'm not interested."

"You can visit other colleges when you come out here. Or help me get Juiced going."

"That's what you're calling it?"

"Think so."

"You know that means getting hammered. Or taking steroids, right?"

"I'll have a built-in client base."

"That's great. I hope it works out, Mom."

"Everything will be fine, Twy. Remember that."

"Why wouldn't everything be fine?"

"Whatever happens. You'll be okay."

Everyone was getting on my nerves.

I hung up with Mom, crawled into bed and retrieved the copy of *Gilgamesh* that Gabriel had given me. It was a page-turner, and I finished the entire poem before going to sleep.

I read about ancient palaces, temples and forests. I read about glory, wealth and power, war and hate, good and evil, and how, by taking one side or another, we miss the truth. At the end I even felt bad for Gilgamesh the tyrant, when he understood that there was no way around death, and that no life was permanent.

What touched me most, though, was the way the epic talked about love. *I will mourn as long as I breathe*, Gilgamesh said about his best friend Enkidu. I understood the nature of such a total love, where only one person could open our minds and hearts. How, through that person alone, we'd know ourselves.

During the night there were loud cracks and crashes, the sound of tree branches breaking like shattering glass. Alarm Ready kept going off, an electronic woman's voice warning everyone to stay indoors.

By dawn she had shut up so I snuck out while Nan slept, creeping onto the hood of the truck and scraping the windshield before rolling down the driveway. On the street I poured melter in front of the wheels and started up the engine.

I drove at twenty miles per hour, passing power lines weighed down by icicles, and military vehicles rescuing stranded cars. Downtown Halo was a deserted ice sculpture.

I pulled onto the highway. Behind the clouds, every so often, there came a bright flash of lightning. Even the Ajax Outlets lot was empty. Any spring crops that had begun growing would be dead, and the farmers would have to start again.

Roads were beginning to clear. Maintenance vehicles had already passed with sand and salt, so I sped up to reach Gabriel.

I unlocked the gate and parked by the barn. After all the crowds and the media, the place seemed too quiet. I yelled and whistled for Storm until I remembered he was with Travis. Gabriel wasn't in the house so I slid through the field to the silo. Even from a distance I could see the damage the ice had caused to the bullet tree. The old oak had lost a lot of branches.

There were no flashlights at the top of the ramp so I felt along the wall as I walked down the tunnel. I called Gabriel's name, but it only echoed back at me in the darkness.

It was a relief to see flickering light coming from the dome. I passed through the entryway and found Gabriel resting on his back. The light turned out to be a dying flashlight on the ground. The electricity and the backup generators were out but Gabriel had still found a way to keep working.

"Hey, lazybones," I said.

He raised an arm a few inches, but the rest of his body didn't move.

That's when I saw his face.

It looked like he was wearing a Halloween mask, his eyes and nose were so swollen. His forehead and cheeks looked like reddish-blue putty, his face and hair crusted in blood, his lip split.

"What happened!" I blurted.

He tried to sit up but yelled out in pain.

"Some admirers came by." His voice was muffled as if his mouth had been stuffed with cotton.

I punched 911 for an ambulance but my phone wouldn't call out. The storm had downed cell towers.

"Can you feel your arms and legs?" I asked, trying not to get hysterical.

"I'm not paralyzed, Twyla." He winced. "Just a little banged up."

"Wait here," I told him.

I ran to the farmhouse and tried the landline but it was dead. When I got into the truck my wheels spun. I had no melter left so I rocked the vehicle like Dad had shown me, but it wouldn't budge. I ran to the barn, falling on the ice over and over again, and found gravel. But the bag was too heavy. I dumped half the contents out, my hands a bloody mess, and dragged what I could to the truck, pouring rocks around the tires until I was able to drive through the field.

It took forever to get him standing. I wrapped his arm around my neck, leaned forward and walked him out of the dome, up the ramp. I don't know how I did it. He weighed so much more than me. He'd take a few steps and I'd drag him, then a few more steps and I'd have to drag him again.

I kept thinking about this schoolyard game, Light as a Feather, Stiff as a Board, where we surrounded a kid and each placed two fingers under his body, chanting, "He's looking ill, he's looking worse, he's dying, he's dead," and then we lifted that body without effort.

"This hurts more than the fight," Gabriel said at one point. "You're breaking more bones."

As I drove to our small hospital, his breathing was labored. He coughed up blood.

I lay on the horn at the Emergency entrance until someone came out. A man in a white uniform peered into the truck, stared at Gabriel and went back inside — not fast enough, I thought — returning with an assistant. He told us there were no stretchers left.

After they helped Gabriel into a wheelchair, I parked and ran inside. The hospital had backup power. I rushed through the sliding doors to the admissions desk and lied on the paperwork, saying I was family. A nurse took me to a waiting area full of people with storm-related injuries.

The phone lines were fine in town. I called Nan and within fifteen minutes she arrived.

"What in the world is going on," she said as she sat beside me.

"Jeremy attacked Gabriel."

"You saw this?"

"We all know he hates him. He's the one who vandalized the mosaic."

"Now hold up," Nan started. "It's dangerous to jump to conclusions. Besides, it could be anyone. There are always haters. Can't count the times we received death threats because of your grandfather's work."

It was a two-hour wait before the doctor came through the double doors.

"He has a concussion. Four rib fractures and a pulmonary contusion, meaning a bruised lung. We've put him on painkillers and something to reduce the swelling, and we're stitching him up." The doctor looked at me. "Bar fight?"

"He was attacked and I know who did it."

"These injuries were caused by blunt trauma," he said. "A weapon was used. You should report this."

"Goddamn right we will."

"Language, Twyla," Nan said. "Can she see him?" she asked the doctor.

"Later on." He gave us a nod and left.

Nan put her arm around me.

"I'm not leaving," I told her.

"Did you call the Finches?"

"Why worry them?"

"Twyla Jane Lee, you call that boy's parents this minute. And another thing." Her worried eyes fell on me. "This is getting out of control. You're too close to the violence. I'm concerned for your safety."

"Make up your mind," I said. "One minute you're gung ho and the next you have it in for him."

"I'm not denying the worth of his artistic endeavor. I hope he wins. We all do. And I can see how he inspires you."

"So *what*, then? What's your point?"

"He's not a humanitarian. There's more going on here."

"He's against the wars. That's why these thugs are beating on him."

"But he participated. And the world he's making in that silo doesn't exist."

"It *did* exist."

"When the contest ends and it's back to reality, what'll you have?"

"I'll have *him*. And he'll have *me*."

"You'll have a Marine battling PTSD. I don't want a sad life for you."

"Just because you have regrets doesn't mean I will," I told her.

"Simmer down, Twyla."

"You simmer down. Gabriel's got more courage than all of us."

"I don't doubt it."

"Then stay out of it."

After our fight, Nan went back to Ash Crescent. I felt thick and rubbery. I was glad to be alone.

I phoned Lucinda and reassured her.

"He's in the hospital but it's just a precaution. Everything's okay."

"The hospital?"

"I'm sure he's been hurt worse in a football game. He needed a few stitches. And they checked for a concussion."

"I don't understand. Gabriel hasn't been in a fight since … was he assaulted?"

"No, no. He's fine."

"Can you put him on?" she asked.

"Tomorrow," I said. "He's asleep." I hadn't looked out for her son. I'd allowed this to happen to him.

I heard Tom Finch interject then. "We should have brought him with us. You never should have supported it, Lucinda."

Gabriel's mother sighed. "I'll phone the hospital and talk to the doctor. See if he thinks we should fly back."

"You know, he has a real shot at winning this. He could save your farm."

"We don't want to save the farm," Lucinda replied. "We realize the mural is important to him. We never said anything so he could finish it. But we'll be listing the property this summer. I've asked Gabriel to join us here. I'm hoping he'll consider it."

32

I was finally nodding off when a nurse came and got me. She
led me to a stuffy room with a row of beds divided by thin,
dingy curtains. Gabriel was at the end of the line near a small
window.

He had a tube stuck in his arm and there were stitches
on his eyebrow and cheekbone. There were bandages on the
bridge of his nose and on his forehead. Ice packs wrapped in
white cloth lay over his ribs.

I pulled a chair up.

"You need a shave," I told him.

"You smell like a barn," he replied. He spoke like he was
short of breath.

"Haven't had time to shower thanks to you. How are you
feeling?"

"Awesome."

"We'll get the cops in. You can identify who did this and
press charges."

"Don't know who it was."

"You didn't see him?"

"Affirmative."

"But you would have heard him coming down the ramp."

"Hearing's not a hundred percent."

"You're a trained Marine."

"I've got no clue who did it. Let's move on."

"It was Jeremy Colt. Jeremy Colt vandalized the mosaic and Jeremy Colt beat you up. With a crowbar, by the looks of it. Why are you protecting him?"

"They came up from behind."

"They?"

"As in him or her. Look, it's no big thing. Just a brush-up. Storm okay?"

"If you hadn't dumped him on Travis, your dog would have protected you."

"You're probably right." He turned his head toward the window that looked onto a wet field of weeds. The post–ice storm landscape was joyless and gray.

"You've had crap luck," I said, my voice unsteady.

He turned to me again. "It hasn't been all bad."

"You got famous these last few days," I told him. "I lost count of the interview requests."

"You do them."

"They want you, not me. You're going to become a great artist, Gabriel. You're going to win and you're going to put the money down on the farm."

"Now she's a fortune teller."

"I was thinking we could convert the barn into a studio, after. For whatever you'll do next."

He rested a finger on my arm. "You're a photographer. Not an assistant."

"Half the space would be mine."

He gave a small laugh. "Course it would."

The nurse came in then. She adjusted the ice packs, ticked off some boxes on her tablet and moved along to the other patients.

"I read *Gilgamesh*," I told him.

"And?"

"Not bad for such an old story."

I looked him over again. It was too much, seeing the old scar and the new wounds, his face all smashed up. I turned away to wipe my eyes.

"Geez. If I'd known it was going to get to you —"

"You have to be in New York by the end of the month," I said.

Gabriel groaned. "We still have to go? Give me a break."

I punched him in the shoulder. "Yes, we still have to go."

"Ouch. Watch it, cowgirl."

They kept him in the hospital for several more days. The doctor said it was precautionary and he told Lucinda that there was no need for them to fly up.

I kept trying to convince Gabriel to report who'd attacked him, and we'd inevitably start arguing. He told me it wouldn't resolve anything. People were bound to have differing opinions and he was ready for it. He wanted to focus on other things. His time was precious, he said.

But I was scared the attackers would come back, and keep coming back until they killed him. Whether it was Jeremy and his buddies, or other townies, or members of the Forces who were against Gabriel's so-called Iraqi-loving mosaic, someone was out to get him.

I also worried about his injuries. Not just the bruised lung and cracked ribs, but also the fact that he kept getting severe headaches. When they came on, he swallowed painkillers and closed his eyes, and his temples and lids would flutter like some internal combat was taking place, until the drugs kicked

in. When I asked what I could do, he only told me that he had
it handled.

I was afraid he'd fall asleep and not wake up because of
some brain injury the medical staff couldn't detect with their
machines. I lay awake at night, terrified that he'd die.

The worst thing was that I couldn't talk with Nan about it.
I told her I was sorry for what I'd said about Grandpa Wallace
and she accepted my apology, but she kept her distance.

The hospital wasn't far from Hawthorn so I visited over the
lunch hours. Sometimes Gabriel was asleep and other times
we talked or sat together without talking.

Everyone in class knew what had happened but no one
asked about it. They just gossiped behind my back.

Billy still wouldn't look at me. Jeremy ignored me, too,
proving his guilt by not hurling his usual insults my way.

Meanwhile Carlos and Hector had taken it upon themselves to stay at the farm gate as security while Trav and Carm
conducted daily tours. We'd all agreed that there never be an
admission fee, and that the mosaic remain free for anyone
wanting to see it. The incentive was in the tips. The crowds
hadn't thinned out. If anything, more people were coming to
Halo.

Gabriel called his parents by phone so that they couldn't
see his face. I'd talk to Lucinda and reassure her while I sat
beside his bed. Then we'd flip through his gigantic book on
Uruk, which he'd had me lug over from the farm, and he'd
point weird and wonderful facts out to me about the world's
first city, where modern Iraq came from.

Gabriel went on about the clay cone mosaic temple there

dedicated to Inanna, or Ishtar, the goddess of love and war.

"Why would a love goddess be a war goddess? It's a contradiction," I told him.

"Love and war only exist together," Gabriel said.

"What are they giving you in here?"

"There wouldn't be war without patriotic love. Both are big on passion and impulse. Both take guts and emotion."

I thought about my parents and my grandparents. "Both destroy."

"Ever the optimist, Twyla Jane Lee."

"Just sayin'."

"And love's a war with yourself." He hesitated. "Ali explained it that way. Said his whole being was at war with himself when he fell for Nasreen. He couldn't own that someone else had become his life's meaning." He gave me a funny look then, and my heart jumped.

He didn't say any more. And I missed my chance to find out what had happened to the interpreter.

One afternoon as I was packing my bag to head back to class, the wiry Marine appeared in the doorway. He was in his civvies but I recognized him anyway.

"Rolo!" Gabriel said and he raised his arm.

"What's going on, Finchy?"

"Just livin' the dream."

Rolo approached with a box of chocolates in one hand and a flowering plant in the other. "You look like hell, dawg. Hope you still got your ugly ass insured."

Gabriel raised a thumb.

Rolo gave him a homie handshake and passed him his tablet. "Got us a new game," he said. "Tank Tours."

"Cool," Gabriel replied, trying to sound upbeat.

"Don't tire him out," I told Rolo.

I put the plant on the windowsill and left so they could catch up.

"Mortar bombs won't land where they're supposed to, see?" I heard Rolo telling Gabriel as I walked away. "The death blossom spray fire's where it's at, bro. Go for the blossoms."

33

By the time Gabriel was discharged from the hospital, the mud flats were drying up, and coyotes appeared in the fields. Crocuses had started blooming on the prairie and the air filled with birdsong.

It was still early morning when we arrived at the farm, but sightseers were waiting at the gate, which Carlos and Hector opened for us. As I pulled up to the barn, Gabriel took in the property and looked out toward the launch pad.

"Everything's the same but different," he said.

His face was healing but the doctor said the fractured ribs would hurt for at least a few more weeks. When he got out of the truck he had to lean on my shoulder. We saw Travis coming through the field with a tour group. He waved as he led the group back to the gate, Storm at his side.

The dog ran over to Gabriel, jumping and barking and wagging his tail, but Gabriel couldn't even bend down to rumple Storm's fur.

Inside, he settled on the couch with his books. The place was spotless and smelled like limes. My guess was that Carm had cleaned the whole house.

Our departure date for New York was coming up and MoMA had sent our itineraries. Friday was our travel day. On

Saturday there was a museum tour in the afternoon, before the gala ceremony. Then we had Sunday morning to do whatever we wanted, before our flight back.

While Gabriel was in the hospital, I'd managed to convince Nan and Dad that the trip was educational, especially since my ticket was paid for by MoMA and I'd only miss a day of school. When Mom told them that I'd stay with her and not at the hotel where Gabriel had a room courtesy of the museum, they gave in.

I had a lot of organizing to do before we left but didn't want to leave Gabriel alone. With Carlos, Hector, Storm and Travis around I knew he was safe, but I still worried. Although the doctor had cleared him for travel after his last scans came back with zero indication of internal damage, his headaches hadn't gone away and I kept catching him zoning out, staring off into space.

"Sure you'll be okay?" I asked.

"Decamp, Twilight. Let me rest."

On my way out, I checked in with Travis by the gate. "How's it going?"

"Haven't had any trouble. We got three visitors' books full of comments. I've got to thank you and Gabriel, Twills. Carm and I've saved enough in tips to pay for half the wedding already."

"Wedding? Way to go, Trav." I hugged him.

He gave me a crooked smile. "We're real pleased."

"Not to change the subject but can you check on him, like, every hour?"

"Sure thing. He's got mail piling up. Looks like fan letters. I've been putting them in his room."

———

I made it through the school days without issue, mainly because Jeremy was often absent. Nobody knew why. He got away with it because Coach Russell invented stories about his football injuries, but Jolene said it was because he had to take care of his dad. If that was the case, I hoped he was suffering, and that he was freaked out about raising Jo's baby.

Gabriel refused to let me visit after class or later in the evenings after my shifts at Taco John's. He said he needed extra sleep before the trip, doctor's orders. He pushed me to catch up on homework and take photos around town. He told me to document Halo for when it would no longer exist.

So I did. I took shots of Luke Pritchett and his lousy cars and balloons. The sad mermaid women at the Sip 'n Sea. The Triple Ds sitting in front of their shabby row houses. Dad and Reg and other riggers at the casinos. Jolene even got me into Sunnyside so I could check out the assembly line.

I photographed Hawthorn kids and the halls and football field, Ajax Outlets, Angstrom from outside the gates, and all our silos from the highway. I photographed Trav and Carm at Tomahawk Mall and I photographed the Exxon and Miss Irene's and the fast-food highway corridor.

Maybe in the future archeologists would study Halo's ruins, just like Uruk.

I didn't have time to develop the film but I labeled and dated the rolls before storing them. They would always be there, even if our town and the people in it disappeared.

In the days leading up to our trip I downloaded maps and apps on tourist attractions in New York, and I put fact sheets about the silo into folders as background information for reporters.

I polished my boots three times over. I packed my cobalt dress for the gala and the Leica and some film.

The night before we left I was too nervous to sleep. To distract myself, I bought some stuff from Walmart and painted my nails and gave my hair a hot oil treatment. I waxed my upper lip, tweezed my eyebrows and shaved my legs. Then I sat at the window till sunup, drinking coffee.

Nan offered to drive us to Shady Springs. We picked Gabriel up in the Airstream early Friday morning. When we arrived at the farmhouse he sat waiting for us on the porch steps. I went to help him over and noticed that he'd combed his hair and shaved again, which must have been painful since he still had bruises and cuts. His jeans and shirt looked new.

He limped to the barn where the Airstream was parked and we climbed into the motorhome.

"Gabriel," Nan nodded. I felt like a kid on a school bus. She'd promised she wouldn't interfere if I let her drive us, but I knew she was still worried.

Gabriel stopped at *Twilight's Last Gleaming* and studied it closely. "It's the plains," he said. "From Viewpoint Boulevard."

"My mom painted it," I told him. "Before she bailed."

"Let's get this show on the road," Nan said. She pulled onto the highway and Leonard Cohen came on full blast.

Nan livened up when Gabriel told her that he had Cohen's poetry books. But he was still on painkillers and within ten minutes he closed his eyes, leaned back and slept most of the way to the airport.

Our travel time was over six hours. We'd have to transfer in Minneapolis.

I'd taken planes before. Once to Philadelphia for an ash-spreading ceremony for Mom's parents, the grandparents I'd never met. And once to Disney World with Nan when I was eight.

Even so, when Gabriel offered me the window seat and we settled in, I didn't realize I was shaking until he put his hand over mine. He'd been working in the silo again. I knew it from the casing cuts — small, red, everywhere — which made it seem like he'd walked through barbed wire.

"Too much coffee," I told him.

"There are worse ways to die," he said.

"That's comforting."

"Where's your camera?" he asked.

I pulled my backpack from under the seat and took out the Leica.

"You going to document this, or what?"

"You'll actually let me take your picture?"

"Why not."

I checked my settings, focused and snapped. "Top three things you want to see in New York?" I asked.

"One, Central Park."

"Including a carousel ride?"

"A carousel ride would not be out of the question."

"Two?"

"The International Center of Photography and also Aperture Foundation." He smiled.

I eyed him suspiciously.

"Some of our country's greatest photo collections are housed there. There's even a school at the ICP."

"How would you know?"

"The programs are expensive but there's scholarships."

"Why is everyone so preoccupied with my education? You forgot Ground Zero."

His smile fell away. "I've seen enough ground zeros."

"But —"

"Don't rip on me. End of discussion."

"No worries," I murmured. "Three?"

"A pie joint," he said. "Your go."

"Grand Central Station, Lady Liberty and a deli."

"The girl knows what she wants."

His face tightened then. He put a hand to one side of his head.

"Does it hurt?" I asked.

"Not in the least."

Soon enough, he swallowed some pills and slept. His breaths were short, probably because of the pain in his ribs. I shot his dry lips, the long lashes of his closed eyes, his bruised face and his scar. I shot his cut hands, and the fragment of ancient script tattooed on his forearm.

I watched two romantic comedies on the trip. In the first film, a boy met a girl, got the girl, lost her and got her back. In the second film, a girl met a boy, got the boy, lost him and got him back.

Both couples couldn't stand each other at first, and it seemed like they had nothing in common. After overcoming many obstacles, in each movie the lovers wound up together. They were meant for each other because their deeply flawed inner selves were the same.

34

I almost wished Mom wasn't meeting us at the airport, so we could wander the city on our own. But she was there all right, with blue streaks in her long black hair, wearing sneakers and leggings and an off-the-shoulder sweatshirt with on-purpose holes in it.

She rushed to hug us and pressed I ♥ NY T-shirts against our chests.

"You look terrible, Gabriel," she told him as she took his duffel and slung it over her shoulder. I offered her my pack but she pushed it back at me. She steered us through the mass of travelers, past digital signs flashing *Welcome to LaGuardia God Bless Our Troops*, to the car park, walking protectively in front of Gabriel while he shrank from the crowds.

Mom's apartment in Queens wasn't far and I caught glimpses of Manhattan from her borough. Gabriel sat in the Honda with his eyes closed but I took in the streets dense with row houses and storefronts, pubs and restaurants, grocers and laundromats, cars and cabs and buses and silver trains, and pedestrians who looked like they came from every part of the world.

It took a while to find parking near Mom's red brick building. We walked a few blocks to her door, the air thick with smells of bakery, fuel, coffee and tobacco.

Her rental was barely bigger than my room at home. The walls were covered in new paintings, mostly skyscrapers in neon hues, and she had one window that looked out onto a fire escape. There was a kitchenette, and a bathroom with a shower but no bath.

When I asked her where she slept she opened the closet door and pulled a mattress down, patting it. "All yours. I'll take the air mattress."

She gave us some of her homemade juice, which tasted surprisingly good. Then we walked to a place called Angelica's. There weren't many people in the dimly lit pizzeria, which I could tell was a relief for Gabriel, as were the booths.

We ordered sodas and then we chose our pie — chicken mozzarella topped with fresh garlic and basil. When it arrived it took up the whole table. I snapped a few shots including one of Gabriel stuffing his face. We ate Nutella calzone for dessert and when the bill came, Gabriel paid and told Mom it was the best pizza he'd ever had.

After that we walked the tree-lined side streets of Sunnyside and Queens Boulevard, from where we could see the Manhattan skyline. The Empire State Building rose above the other high-rises like a missile.

"Are you nervous about tomorrow?" Mom asked Gabriel.

"I was worried about not finishing," he replied. "What comes next isn't as important. I mean, the money would be nice."

Mom nodded. "Ever find out who vandalized the mosaic?"

Gabriel paused. "No, ma'am."

"Twyla tells me you didn't see your attacker, either."

"That's correct."

"Props for not letting it get to you." Mom studied him.

A cool breeze picked up and Gabriel checked the time.

"I should head for the hotel," he told us. We walked back to the apartment, and I went up to get his bag so he wouldn't have to climb the stairs again.

"I'll drive you," Mom was offering when I came back down.

"I'd like to take the subway. Get the real experience," Gabriel said, heaving his duffel over his shoulder.

"There's cab money in your per diem," I told him. "Save your energy."

When he declined, we said goodnight and Mom directed him to the trains.

Back inside, we changed into our pajamas and sat on the loveseat by the window with a bowl of M&M's. Mom turned out the lights and lit a candle.

"Do you like it here?" I asked her.

"I'm content enough."

"Dad misses you."

"Same."

"So why'd you leave?"

"I can't remember anymore."

The light from the skyline filtered in through the iron staircase.

"You should paint that," I told her.

I only woke up when I heard the door unlock and Mom coming in with bagels and coffee. I packed what I'd need for the day and evening into one of her big purses.

"Keep me posted," she said, kissing me on the forehead.

I left for the subway to meet Gabriel. It was exhilarating to travel with so many strangers. The best part was that I didn't know anyone and nobody knew me.

I waited for him at the information booth at the center of Grand Central's main concourse, by an opal-faced clock. The terminal was a huge echoing space with tall arched windows and chandeliers. A large American flag hung before me, bigger even than the one at Halo's Walmart. The ceiling was a blue-green night sky with the constellations of the zodiac painted in gold, and standing there beneath it I got the same feeling as when I'd first stood inside the silo.

You could hear the rumbling of the trains. I shot the throngs of people moving in waves around me. I knelt and focused on the legs and feet rising and falling like a pulse, going anywhere and everywhere, until two feet appeared that I recognized.

"Where would you go?" he asked as we scanned destinations on the boards displaying times and track numbers of arriving and departing trains.

"Here," I told him.

"I'd go to Montauk," he said. "I hear the fishing's good there."

"We've got an hour before the tour." I looked up things to see in the station on my phone. "Let's visit the Kissing Room."

We walked over to the Biltmore Room, also called the Kissing Room, a spot near some tracks where people once reunited with loved ones after getting off long-distance trains. Families and lovers also waited there for arriving military troops. But we didn't see any kissers, only a Starbucks and a flower shop.

"I guess it's not a meeting place anymore," I said, disappointed.

There was one other place I wanted to see. It was called the Whispering Galley.

We walked down a ramp, deeper into the station.

I led him to the tiled chamber by the oyster bar. Because of the height, size and curve of the arches in this space, if you stood in one corner and whispered into the wall, and had the person you were with stand across the underpass, they could hear you.

I explained what we had to do.

"When I get over there," I pointed, "turn into the corner and whisper me something." I had to yell through the crowds of tourists.

I went across the chamber and strained to hear his voice in a multitude of other voices and people passing. When he finally spoke, though, I heard it clearly, like we were standing face to face.

"It's a good day, Twilight."

"Most definitely," I whispered back.

I took Gabriel's picture in front of Grand Central. Then we got hot dogs from a stand and walked to MoMA, fifteen minutes away. A lot of the food trucks we went by had signs on them that said, *Owned and Operated by US Army Disabled Vet*, but Gabriel didn't comment on it or talk to any of the guys.

All of Manhattan seemed to be under construction. There were crews and cranes, scaffolding and sidewalk sheds everywhere. Eventually we stopped trying to talk over the digging and drilling and jackhammering.

The museum took up more than half a city block and was bigger than a battleship.

We passed through some revolving doors and approached the information desk to ask about our tour. We'd arrived late, and the group had left without us.

"Good," Gabriel said. "Let's explore."

The museum had six floors.

"Where to?" I asked. "We only have a couple of hours."

"Let's each choose a few things."

I'd downloaded the highlights app. "Monet's water lilies?" I suggested.

221

We climbed some stairs, then went up an escalator. Gabriel studied my phone and led me through the galleries as I scanned the walls and tried to take in all the art, until we arrived at the painting. A crowd wearing headphones stood in front of three immense panels, but we found a bench and sat down until the group moved along.

Like the gold from the Great Plains dipping into the horizon, you couldn't tell where the lilies, the sky above, the water and the clouds began or ended. There was something mesmerizing about the painting, and Gabriel seemed calmer sitting there. Almost at peace.

He rolled his brochure into a scope and looked through it.

"Should've saved this for last," he finally said. Then, "How about we check out the fourth floor? I heard someone call it crackbrained."

We went back down the escalator and walked through rooms of things from the 1960s. Fake rocks, an ice-cream-cone pillow, a weight scale, a TV turned on its side and fluorescent light tubes. Apparently all were considered art.

Then Gabriel stopped at a clear acrylic chair with roses suspended in it. The roses were thick and deep red. They looked like trapped hearts, beating and alive.

"I love that!" I exclaimed. Light passed through the chair so that silhouettes of the roses projected onto the ground.

I noticed him wincing like he had a headache again.

"Want to sit?" I asked.

He shook his head. "No rest for the wicked."

The photography galleries on the third floor were closed for reinstallation so we walked through a temporary display of photos instead. The people in the glossy shots looked like models from fashion magazines. It wasn't all that impressive.

So we went back to the fifth floor to look at more paintings and sculptures.

Gabriel reviewed the app again.

"Let me introduce you to Jackson Pollock," he said, stopping before a loopy colored canvas of drips and spills of paint labeled *One: Number 31, 1950.*

"He sure went all out naming it," I said. "Seems to me anyone could do this."

"You try when we get home, hotshot."

The more I looked at the painting, the more complicated it seemed. It reminded me of the mosaic in its movement and rhythm, and in its feeling of chaos and order combined.

We walked through other rooms, slowing here and there until we ended up in front of a still life with fruit, goblets and puppies.

"I've never understood what they mean by still life," I told him. "Does it mean life's gone still and all the stuff in these pictures is dead or dying? Or is it saying, here's life frozen for a bit? Or does it mean more, like, even with all the crap going on in the world, still, there is life, and here it is?"

"I like your last interpretation. Still, there is life."

Gabriel told me to close my eyes and hold his arm. I leaned against him as we took a few slow steps, and my heartbeat drowned out the noise of the tour groups.

When he stopped he stayed close beside me.

"You can look now," he said.

Colors and movement swirled before me in a thick, wavelike night sky of exploding stars and a bright moon, over hills and a town with a church and steeple, and the dark green shadow of a large tree.

"This is what Van Gogh saw at twilight," he told me. "They say he sold only one known painting during his life."

I read the label. *This morning I saw the country from my window a long time before sunrise, with nothing but the morning star, which looked very big.*

The scene reminded me of Halo before it deteriorated and got rundown.

This was the perfect ending to our tour. Me, Gabriel and *The Starry Night.*

On our way out we visited the garden, a room without a ceiling. The sun was out and we ate gelato and looked at the sculptures in among the trees and water court. By then we only had two hours left before the gala.

"Let's hit the hotel," he said.

Outside the museum someone was replacing the afternoon events banner with a banner announcing the award night, with photos of each artist and their works, but he was too embarrassed to let me take his picture in front of it.

As we headed toward the hotel, Mom phoned to check in and to wish Gabriel good luck. Nan texted, and so did Dad. Lucinda also called.

Then Gabriel switched his ringer off. And so I switched mine off, too.

They were putting him up at the Waldorf Astoria. Each artist was designated a hotel tied to their work. Elizabeth had let us know that they'd picked the Waldorf for Gabriel because of its mosaic tile floor.

When we turned in at the hotel, a doorman opened the gleaming glass and brass door for us. The lobby was like something from a movie, with ancient-looking murals and columns and giant vases. I felt like a hick among the rich travelers.

We stood in the center of the mosaic floor, a big circle called the "Wheel of Life." Gabriel said it portrayed our existence from birth to death. Like in the murals, the people in the mosaic looked ancient.

"I assume you got the lowdown from the concierge?" I said.

Gabriel nodded as we turned inside the circle.

"One, a happy family when their baby's born. Two, youth and friendship. Three, life struggles. Four, love. Five, wisdom and old age. Six, death."

"That's all there is to it?"

"If you're lucky. If you get that far."

As we stood there, people walked across the mosaic without noticing it.

Gabriel's room was high up. I pulled the curtains back on tall buildings in all directions.

He got a beer from the mini bar and poured me a glass of wine. We sipped our drinks and took in the view.

"Do you think New York will sink one day, like Venice?" I asked, looking down at a stream of cabs and cars and black SUVs.

"Probably."

"Thoughts on the city so far?" I asked.

"There's less sky and light. Less air."

I kicked my boots off and pulled the cobalt dress from my bag. It was extremely wrinkled.

I sighed. "I so don't feel like ironing."

"Stand in the shower with me," Gabriel said.

I felt dizzy then.

"I mean, put it on and stand at the vanity while I shower. Creases'll disappear."

I put the dress on and went into the bathroom. He'd draped a towel over the shower door but I could still see his bare legs and his arms when he raised them, until the room steamed up.

It was impossible not to imagine his body as I tried to untangle my hair and smooth it into a bun.

I was applying my makeup when the water stopped. I didn't move or breathe as he reached for the towel and wrapped it around his waist.

"How are your ribs?" I asked, trying to keep my voice steady as I collected my things and moved to the mirror in the bed-room.

"Better."

"And your headache?"

"Twyla. Stop."

But I couldn't. He never had headaches before the beating. And he still struggled to take deep breaths. I was paranoid that Gabriel had internal injuries in his lungs or brain.

I finished doing my eyeshadow and put on the earrings and necklace Mom had given me to match the dress.

Gabriel emerged from the bathroom in his suit.

I stood there in my dress.

"Wow," he said.

"Same to you."

He grabbed his wallet, phone and room card. We were run-ning late.

The air was crisp, the construction noise had subsided and the sidewalks had emptied out of daytime workers. We saw the moon reflected in the buildings as we walked. From a block away we could see streams of hip-looking twenty- and thirty-somethings filing into MoMA.

Gabriel stopped and turned to face me.

"So. This is it," he said.

I nodded. "This is it."

I hooked my arm through his and we walked together into the museum's brightness.

35

The gala was happening in the Atrium on the second floor, an enormous cube of a space with no art. Maybe the room was the art. Soon after we got there, the lights went off and blue strobing and pulsing kicked in all around us. A spotlight hit the wall behind the stage, where images of the finalists' work were projected.

It was an hour before the ceremony and the place was already packed. We noticed Zohar Berkowitz right away, scowling in a corner by a harp player. Then we spotted Renny, this time in red jeans and a black shirt and tie, surrounded by groupies.

Elizabeth Malone approached us near the bar. She looked like an exotic bird in a gown made from feathers.

"Gabriel! Twyla! Welcome." She led us over to the other two finalists.

Lori Smith, the labyrinth artist, was a middle-aged woman with thinning hair and black-rimmed glasses, who wore skinny jeans and a blouse. She looked more like she was on her way to the library than to a gala. She made me feel comfortable right away.

"Great to finally meet you, Gabriel." She shook our hands. "Love your mosaic. It's very Ai Weiwei."

Matthew Friesen wasn't as friendly. He was young and looked like the sharks in his painting, with small, far-apart eyes and pointy teeth.

"Good luck," was all he said.

Elizabeth took the three of them to the banner at the entrance of the Atrium for photos. Then they were directed to separate galleries for interviews with arts reporters.

Before she left with him I gave her my camera.

"Can you take our picture?" I asked. "Just press here." I dragged Gabriel back to the banner.

"Move closer together," she said. "Put your arm around her, Gabe."

Gabriel slipped his arm around my waist as the shutter clicked and the flash went off. I asked her to take a few more, just in case. I looked up at Gabriel at the same time as he looked down to me.

"Lovely," Elizabeth said and snapped again before she handed back the Leica and led Gabriel away.

"Good luck," I told him as I watched him go, my voice uneven. "Break a leg."

"Haven't I had enough injuries?" he called back to me. "What kind of an agent are you?"

I filled up on finger food, then went up to the fifth floor, kept open specially for the event, to calm myself down. I was a wreck. This was the life-changing moment that would define his future. Our future.

We would live on the farm. I'd distract him from his dark war thoughts, and I'd manage his career. We'd make art together. And maybe babies, one day.

As I wandered through the rooms, I didn't see anything remotely resembling the mosaic. No one had done what Gabriel had done. Sure, artists used ammo in art. But that was like saying that Van Gogh and Jackson Pollock both used paint.

In Gallery 10, around the corner from the Pollock, I stopped at an oil painting called *The Persistence of Memory* by Salvador Dalí. The painting was so small I'd missed it the first time. It was of a barren sci-fi landscape with no humans, just a dead tree, toxic-looking water and a cliff. There were melting clocks draped here and there and a gruesome face in the center of it all. I couldn't get the picture out of my head even after I'd moved on. Maybe because the painting represented a farewell to the world as we knew it.

I went back to the Atrium, sat on a bench and smoothed my dress. I watched the elegant people around me. Then I called Nan. She told me she'd just finished installing surround sound in the Airstream.

"Ready to hit the road?" I asked.

"Once I see my granddaughter graduate."

"You name it yet?"

"I'm counting on you for that. How's Gotham?"

"Winner's going to be announced soon."

"You got an envelope from UCLA in the mail yesterday."

"Thanks."

"This one's thin. Want me to open it?"

"Sure."

"You didn't get in."

"Huh."

"At least pretend to care."

"I should go."

She sighed. "Twinks ..."

"Yeah?"

"My feelings about you two aside, the boy's an artist."

I looked toward the stage and saw that Elizabeth, Renny and Zohar were already leading the finalists onto the platform.

My stomach tightened. As Elizabeth approached the podium I hopped up and down in the crowd, waving frantically
at Gabriel until he spotted me and waved back.

Elizabeth raised a feathered arm to get everyone's attention.

She introduced MoMA as a 21st-century think tank for art,
and she talked about artists who turn your world upside down
and inside out, questioning the universe around them.

Then Renny went on about what makes art art. He talked
about the art of our time, citing examples of his own work,
and he discussed innovation and experiment and what moved
him. He looked directly at Gabriel when he said this.

Zohar was up next. He explained the judges' analytical
breakdown, including the importance of form, meaning and
function, cultural impact, process and necessity.

Then some board members and sponsors came onstage
with a gigantic replica of a hundred-thousand-dollar check,
with the recipient's name missing.

"What will you do with the money!" someone asked from
the audience.

Matthew Friesen answered without hesitating. "I've drafted
blueprints to renovate my studio with climate control and a
sauna."

"Find my dad a nice home," Lori Smith said. "He's got de-
mentia. With what's left I'd buy supplies. Not that I've thought
any of this out," she added, and the crowd laughed.

Everyone's attention turned to Gabriel. He gave a small cough.

"Pay down the farm," he said.

"What's your next project?" someone asked.

"This was it," he told them. "I'm a one-trick pony."

"We don't believe you!" someone else called out.

Elizabeth leaned into the microphone again. "Without further ado, ladies and gents."

She held her breath as she opened the envelope.

"Each finalist captured our imaginations and left us hungry for more," she said. "Their works are dynamic and limitless. They've ventured into a new era. Most importantly, they provoked thoughts and feelings in us that we've never experienced before."

Gabriel stared at his feet. Matthew burned holes into Elizabeth Malone's back. Lori looked up at the ceiling like she was praying.

"The second runner-up of the Museum of Modern Art's tenth installment of America's Next Great Artist — sponsored by Bloomberg, Forbes, Goldman Sachs and Hyundai Capital America. We applaud the commitment made by our corporate sponsors who have made this competition possible each year. And the winner of five thousand dollars is Matthew Friesen!"

Matthew's lips thinned as Elizabeth stepped aside and Renny approached the microphone.

"And the first runner-up of the Museum of Modern Art's tenth installment of America's Next Great Artist, and the winner of ten thousand dollars, is Gabriel Finch!"

Elizabeth stepped in again. "Which means that our winner is Lori Smith!"

Applause broke out as Elizabeth turned to hug Lori. Renny shook Matthew's and Gabriel's hands, and Zohar gave them each an envelope and ushered them offstage.

Lori was in tears as the sponsors and board members stood with her before the cardboard check, which now included her name, for pictures.

When Elizabeth had said his name, for a fraction of a second I thought he was the winner. I'd led Gabriel to think that he'd win and he'd believed me. I'd believed it myself. And now it was over. I pushed my way through the crowd to reach him.

231

He was surrounded by people congratulating him and had to excuse himself to come over to me.

"Let's get out of here," he said, grabbing my hand.

As we headed for the exit, Elizabeth called after him. We stopped and waited as she rushed up to us.

"Often the first runner-up gets as much attention and offers as the winner," she told him. "We'll feature your mosaic online all month. And I've taken the liberty of contacting Guinness World Records. They'll be paying Halo a visit." She waved goodbye and flitted back to the Atrium.

"Guinness World Records in Halo. Who would've thought." Gabriel turned to me, smiling.

I felt sick inside.

"Now what?" I asked.

"Now we have fun," he said. "I'm starving. Let's get something to eat."

36

Not far from the museum we found a deli and ordered corned beef sandwiches on rye. We ate on stools at the window. Gabriel urged me to take photos of people walking by, but my heart wasn't in it. My disappointment was gradually being replaced by a rising sense of panic that when we got back to Halo, the Finches would list the farm and Gabriel would be left with nowhere to go and no place to live.

He didn't seem worried, sitting there on his stool, watching New Yorkers from inside the warm deli.

Every once in a while, though, he rubbed at his temples like his head hurt.

"You deserved to win," I told him.

He finished his sandwich and set his basket aside.

"We're ten grand richer than we were an hour ago," he smiled.

"Can you slap that on the farm? Buy some time?"

"Don't think that'll cut it."

I adjusted his suit jacket, which he'd put around my shoulders when we were still outside.

"We can save the farm some other way," I said. "You've got fans now. People will help."

"As luck would have it, my parents don't want to save it. I'm not sure I want to either."

"By saving the farm I mean saving the mosaic."

"The silo belongs to the Forces. I always knew that."

"So where does that leave you? With alpacas in Peru?"

"Can you see me as an alpaca farmer?" he asked, and we laughed.

Mom texted then. She said to tell Gabriel he was a winner to us, and told me to have my butt back to her place by eleven.

"We've got two hours," I told him.

"We're ten minutes from Central Park," he said.

We bought a bottle of sparkling wine at a corner store and walked to 59th and 6th, where a line of horses and carriages waited.

"I know it's corny," I said. "But just humor me, okay?"

"The girl has seen one too many Hollywood flicks," he apologized to the driver as he paid him. "But I'm looking forward to sitting down again."

Even at night Central Park hummed. Dog walkers and joggers passed us as pools of lamplight unveiled deep-green rocky slopes, winding paths and stone archways. The slow clip-clopping of the horses was restful. We rode by a group of break-dancers and couples on benches and a police patrol car. Beyond the trees, the skyline view was surreal. The carousel was closed, but we rode around the outside anyway. Every so often the driver pointed out landmarks that we couldn't quite see in the dark — the Chess and Checkers House, Sheep Meadow, the zoo and the pond.

Eventually we got off where we got on. The driver gave me a carrot to feed the horse, and he offered to take our picture when he saw my camera. I adjusted the settings and passed it to him. He snapped just as the horse put its soft nose on Gabriel's cheek.

It was time for me to get back. Gabriel hailed a cab. Then out of nowhere he drew me in and kissed me, and neither of us pulled away or ended it too soon.

"Sweet dreams," was all he said. His white scar glowed like a crescent moon on his skin.

It didn't feel like our first kiss. It felt like we'd been kissing since before even Uruk existed.

On Sunday morning we made plans to meet at Battery Park and head to the airport from there.

"I've hardly seen you," Mom complained.

"We'll be back," I told her. "Gabriel likes it here. The art, I mean. Not the crowds."

"Tell me, Twy. What is it about him, aside from the intense feelings?"

"He gets me. He makes me feel good about who I am."

"You don't need someone else to do that for you."

"You don't understand," I told her. I looked down at my camera, fiddling with the focusing wheel of my lens until I came to the sideways 8. "He's my infinity."

When I arrived at Battery Park I found Gabriel sitting by the water near an old clipper sailboat, staring out at Lady Liberty. I sat beside him on the bench and he handed me a coffee.

"She's smaller than I thought she'd be," I commented.

"Bit of a letdown."

"Want to take the ferry to get a closer look?" I asked.

"Not really," he said.

"Same here."

Some uniformed guys with cameras around their necks passed by.

"It's a short walk to the Memorial," I said.

"Nah. I'm good."

Boat horns went off in the distance and a helicopter circled over the choppy water. The air smelled like the ocean.

He pointed to what I thought was garbage, next to the bench.

"Got you something."

I pulled a black bag off a large object, which turned out to be the chair with roses inside it, from the museum.

"Don't worry, I didn't steal it. Gift-shop replica." He repositioned the chair to a spot where the sun shone, so that the roses cast shadows onto the walkway. "Have a seat."

I sat down and looked out at the green statue on her podium with her torch, then at Gabriel.

"Thank you," I told him, and he nodded.

With what time remained, Gabriel wanted to visit photo galleries, but a lot of them were closed on Sundays.

Finally we carried the chair to a small gallery a few blocks away. There were barely a dozen other visitors.

The exhibition presented a street photographer named Vivian Maier, who took something like 200,000 photos during her lifetime.

Maier worked as a nanny for over forty years, and she was unknown and penniless at the end of her life. Her pictures were only discovered when the contents of an abandoned storage unit were auctioned off.

She photographed maids, the homeless, street kids, housewives, crooks. There was a gripping beauty to her black-and-white shots of people caught off guard.

For the first time ever, I understood photography as art.

Along with the hoard of negatives, Maier left audio recordings behind. We approached the speaker and Gabriel pressed the button.

Well, I suppose nothing is meant to last forever. We have to make room for other people. It's a wheel. You get on, you have to go to the end. And then somebody has the same opportunity to go to the end and so on.

It was just like the mosaic at the Waldorf Astoria. It was just like what the *Epic of Gilgamesh* said.

37

Nan didn't ask about the contest on the drive back to Halo. I knew that in her mind, losing was what she called a Cadillac problem: a problem that wasn't a problem in the grand scheme of things.

Passing ranches and pastures of grazing livestock, she glanced at us both in the rearview mirror from time to time.

Eventually she turned down her music.

"There was a lineup, an actual lineup, outside Michelle's Diner the other day. And that's not all."

Gabriel watched a cargo train in the distance.

"What else?" I asked.

"Word is, there are other vets making mosaics in decommissioned Typhons around these parts now."

Gabriel looked at Nan, bewildered.

"You've inspired them," she told him. "That alone's worth more than some check."

She focused on the highway again and turned her music up.

Gabriel went back to staring out the window.

"You hear that?" I shook his shoulder.

He turned to me. "I've been having this dream where I'm filling craters. Hundreds of them. Our gravel roads remind me of the dream."

"I have a plan," I told him.

"Which I guess I'm about to hear."

"Buy your parents out. You couldn't have a more spacious studio. For land art, even!"

"With what money?"

"Start with the ten grand. Then we'll do an online campaign to raise funds."

"I'm not a charity case."

"Get off your high horse. This is an entrepreneurial proposition. We'll keep general entries free, then offer a paid tour with all the silos, seeing as there'll be more of them. We'll make maps and brochures. We'll have a website. Each stop will have a different theme." I was getting more and more excited. "We could charge at least fifty bucks a head. Not to mention that once Guinness comes, and you get into World Records ..." I was practically jumping off the seat.

He took a deep breath as we pulled onto the dirt road leading to the farm. That meant his ribs were healing. And I hadn't seen him wincing the whole drive home.

While Nan wasn't looking, he kissed the inside of my wrist, then pressed his hand on mine.

"I can't do it," he said.

He threw his duffel bag over his shoulder and thanked Nan before he stepped down from the Airstream.

"Yes, you can!" I hollered.

I figured he was just tired. As I watched him walk to the farmhouse, I knew he'd come around.

I focused on finishing school, motivated by the fact that as soon as I graduated, I could concentrate on saving the farm with Gabriel. In class I ignored everyone, including Jeremy and Jolene, and Billy. In my free time I put all my energy into studying.

Guinness World Records contacted us and made an appointment to visit Halo, to count the cartridges and casings in the mosaic. They told us that Gabriel's entry would simply be titled, *World's Largest Ammunition Mosaic.*

The mountains were still covered in snow but our landscape was greening, warm winds had arrived, and wildflowers grew everywhere. Even the stars were brighter.

Aside from the milder weather, another new development filled me with hope. The times I stopped by the farm before or after tour hours to hang out with Gabriel, he didn't drink beer or pop pills. Instead I'd find him working out, running laps in the field, doing pushups and crunches near the barn, or jogging up and down the staircase in the house. He hardly limped anymore.

Then one afternoon when I went over after class, I noticed a Marine-issued Humvee among the other cars parked at the gate. As I was getting out of the truck, Muscle Face and Rolo came out of the house.

"It's Finchy. Course he can," Rolo said.

"Pay's too good to turn down." Muscle Face folded his cannon-like arms as I stepped onto the porch.

"Hey there," I said. "What's going on?"

"We came by to see the mosaic," Rolo said, looking on edge as usual.

"Great. I finished my volunteer hours, by the way."

"Good going." Rolo went in for a fist pound.

"You'll get the forms by end of term."

"Roger that." Muscle Face saluted me.

"You guys have no idea what I'm talking about, do you."

They looked at each other, then at me.

"You're not from the Help a Vet program, are you?"

"We're just here visiting our buddy."

So no one from Help a Vet had ever come to check in on Gabriel. Not once.

I raised my arms and made the peace sign with both hands as they drove off.

Gabriel stood inside the doorway like he'd been waiting for me. He had this look on his face that made me catch my breath, even though I couldn't quite read it.

As he sat beside me I glanced at the coffee table and noticed a piece of paper on top of some books. I absentmindedly picked it up, thinking at first that it was a blackout poem because lines were crossed out here and there. There were scribbled words about "Prior active service," "special duty," "Sept latest," "Deployment," and "Zone 2 yr re-enlist".

"What's this?" I asked.

Gabriel took the paper from my hand and studied it like he'd never seen it before.

"Nothing important," he said.

"It's your handwriting."

"I made notes, chatting with the guys."

"Why?" Alarm bells sounded in my head.

He reached for my arm.

"What aren't you telling me?" I asked, pulling away.

And the way he looked at me then, I knew.

The room went blurry.

"They won't take you," I whispered. I could barely hear myself. "There's no way."

"They'll take anyone these days." He tried to laugh but his voice cracked. "Controlled meds are permitted, and my hearing's better. I've got pills for the arthritis."

I backed away. "When did you decide this?"

"I wanted to tell you sooner ..."

None of it made sense. I went to the window and put my forehead on it, fighting the urge to smash my fist through the glass.

"You knew you'd go back?"

"I didn't think we'd get this close. By the time we did ... the contest was so important to you. And you wanted to see New York so much."

My insides had gone completely numb.

"I didn't care about New York," I told him, my voice shrill in my ears. "I wanted *you*. I wanted *us*."

But there was no "us." There hadn't been enough time for "us" to exist. Us was the next step, and now it would never come to that.

The signs had been in my face since the beginning. Being in such a hurry to finish the mosaic. Running laps to keep in shape. The visits from his platoon buddies and not caring if the farm went into foreclosure. And, worst of all, giving up his own dog.

Then I thought I understood.

"The Forces are blackmailing you. Did they say they'd implode the silo if you don't re-enlist? So it doesn't seem like you're against the cause? So you don't give them a bad rap?"

He shook his head.

Then he put a hand on my waist and I didn't have the energy to push it off, my shoulders shaking.

"Why?" I pleaded. "You said it's useless."

"We haven't delivered on what we promised."

"Then you're an idiot. And you'll fail."

"Maybe."

"You're wasting your life. Nothing will change."

"I have to make things right."

"How? You can't make civilians undead, Gabriel."

"Listen to me, Twyla. I want to be with you."

"So *be* with me."

"When I come back."

But I couldn't hear what he was saying. I couldn't get past my shock.

Gabriel had always intended to return to the wars, whether he won the contest or not.

I looked out at the gnarled bullet tree. He reached an arm out and laced his fingers through mine. I could hardly breathe.

"I can't move on if I don't do this."

"So that's it, then. That's your choice?"

He watched me and waited. I knew then that a part of him had stayed in the wars all along.

"You can't have it both ways. Just like you can't fix what you've done. Don't you get it?" I forced myself to stop crying and pulled my hand away. I grabbed my bag in the living room and kicked over his stack of books on ancient, ruined places.

"I never want to see you again," I told him, and I left.

38

In June I turned eighteen. Mom, Dad and Nan pooled together
and bought me a German Rolleiflex, a medium-format twin-
lens reflex. It was an older model like the one Vivian Maier
would have used. The camera gave square frames on a roll and
loading was easy and quick, making it ideal for action and street
shots. I opened the gift and we ate birthday cake and phoned
Mom. I pretended to be excited.

Then I told them that I was leaving Halo. I wasn't sure how
or where I'd go, but I was going. I asked Nan if I could join her
on her trip, but she said no. And I couldn't imagine attending
college. My last resort was to move to New York and stay with
Mom for a while.

They knew that Gabriel and I were through. And nobody
said I told you so, after I owned up that he'd re-enlisted for
another tour.

I no longer went to the farm.

Meanwhile, Travis kept updating me on Guinness World
Record's imminent visit. Gabriel had given him and Carm use
of the land to manage the mosaic as a tourist site, and to house
Trav's pets and Storm. They were living there full-time, off
tips and donations, which would increase during the summer
months. The money coming in even covered the minimum

mortgage payments. I told Travis that I was thrilled for him, but that I didn't want to hear about the mosaic anymore. I was able to take over as manager at Taco John's until I could save up enough to move away.

Final exams were in two weeks. Everyone in class was jacked up about graduating and the day came where we handed in our community service hours.

When I brought my paperwork to Hooper's desk, she looked at me attentively.

"Twyla Jane Lee," she said. "Any last thoughts?"

"I'm glad it's over," I told her, returning to my seat.

Jolene harassed me to meet up with her after class. She said she had something to show me. I thought it was related to the baby, so I decided not to deprive her because her life was about to start sucking badly.

When I stopped in at Le Paris, she led me to her room and closed the door. She sat down on her bed and made me sit beside her.

"Don't flip out," she said.

She scrolled through her phone until she located a video.

"I found this on Jer's tablet when I was making sure he wasn't surfing porn." She handed it over.

It was hard to see anything at first. The filmer was going down the silo ramp. I recognized Jeremy's voice, then saw him stepping into the dome.

"Mofo thinks he'll hit pay dirt with this camel jockey crap." There was someone beside him but I couldn't make out who it was.

So there were three of them. Jeremy, the filmer and another person. My guess was Michael Kemp and Troy Whitman.

Gabriel was crouched down, sorting through ammo. Music was playing, something slow and classical. Jeremy tapped

Gabriel on the shoulder and let him stand up before he punched him. Then they both went at it.

It was an even fight at first, until Billy stepped into the frame, a beer bottle in one hand and a baseball bat in the other.

"Have at 'er," Jeremy told him as he pinned Gabriel's arms behind his back.

Billy tossed his bottle aside and stepped in close to Gabriel, raising the bat and slamming it into his chest. Gabriel fell to his knees and Jeremy kept his arms in a tight hold.

Then Billy dropped the bat and turned to go, but Jeremy yelled, "Go for it, Goodwin. Teach him a lesson." So Billy punched Gabriel in the face and in the head, over and over again, while Jeremy hooted and hollered, until Billy slurred, "Enough. Move it out."

Then the screen went black.

I was mad at myself for not suspecting Billy, especially after Yellowstone. I handed the phone to Jolene.

"See," she said. "Jer didn't do it."

I looked at her with disbelief. "You're dumber than I thought, Jo."

"Why?" she asked, her voice quivering. "This proves it was Billy."

There was no point explaining to her that Jeremy was just as guilty, like overlooking the generals and politicians running the wars from their control rooms.

"I don't care," I told her. "None of this is my problem any-more."

"What d'you mean?"

I bit the inside of my cheek. "He re-enlisted."

"I know. Jer's going, too." Jolene chewed on her nails.

I got up to leave. "Can you forward me that video?"

"You'd only take it to the cops. I need him around, Twy."

I nodded at her growing stomach. "How does Jackie feel about being a grandma?"

She shook her head. "Says I'm eating like a cow."

I left Jolene's and drove to Affinity. Billy opened the door and Jeremy came up behind him.

"I saw the video. That's assault with a deadly weapon. And the graffiti ... these are hate crimes," I told them.

Jeremy stared me down. "A homo like him doesn't need you fighting his battles. Let him come after us if he wants. His colossal screw-up on mission is what gives Marines a bad name."

I wanted to tear his face off, and Billy's, too. I didn't even recognize myself anymore. "Fuck off, Jeremy."

"You fuck off. He loves towelheads so much he can't even shoot their Islamic Staters. He deserved it."

I started walking away.

"Don't you want to hear what your loverboy did?" he taunted.

I turned back to face him and crossed my arms.

"He got too chummy with one of *them*," he started. "His platoon's terp. Who, it turns out, had this jihadist cousin. When the cousin found out the terp worked for us, he strapped explosives onto a freaking kid. Then he wrangles up the rest of them, the ones he called traitors, including the terp and his ho."

I couldn't tell if he was making it up.

"And they all approach checkpoint arm in arm, right? And everyone at first thinks it's cool, that the terp's coming to say, hey, meet my wifey, meet my family, till they see it's not cool."

I realized I was grinding my jaw and stopped myself.

"Cousin's crouching behind the kid, holding the detonator. Finch doesn't fire. Just stands there looking from the kid to the terp. So they all get blown to bits. BOOM!"

The air was mild but I started shivering. I left and didn't look back.

I parked at Hill 5 and sat in the grass. Angstrom looked like a ghost town. All the families had relocated. There were no armored vehicles driving up and down the streets anymore, no drills, no sound of fighter jets.

Within a month, the carefully cut and watered lawns and other green spaces inside the grid would dry out. The roads would crack, and all the little houses would shift and sink in on themselves until Angstrom disappeared, a rusted metal fence with nothing inside it.

I wondered how much of what Jeremy said was true. It made me sick to think that Gabriel had been put in such a nightmarish position. Then I remembered how he'd decided to pattern the silo's ceiling and floor and ramp. It hadn't occurred to me that he'd run out of room as body counts increased.

Soon he'd be off to Fort Stelan for training.

He didn't call or stop by. He'd completely respected my wishes when I told him I never wanted to hear from him again. Where Gabriel was concerned it was dead air, like he'd never existed in the first place.

39

Not breaking with tradition, at the end of term recruiting officers came through Hawthorn High like the pied piper. They offered college scholarships after time served. They offered subsidized food, housing and education, health care, vacation time, bonus pay, special pay and cash allowances.

Then, on the last day of class, Hooper distributed cupcakes and assigned us the final task of our high-school careers.

"Write a letter to yourself ten years from now," she told us. "And I'll mail it to you."

Exams came and went and I didn't do any better or worse than usual.

Mom flew out for graduation. At the ceremony, she and Dad and Nan clapped and cheered and gave me flowers. We went to the dinner and I didn't dance with anyone aside from Dad.

Later that night Jolene begged me to go with her to the post-grad barnburner. Jeremy was stuck with his dad and she wanted a lift, even though she couldn't booze it up anymore.

There were former Hawthorn grads at the party, including Marines. I spotted Rolo almost straight away.

"Remember me?" I asked.

He sat alone on a log, drinking from a plastic cup and staring into the bonfire.

"Sure." He extended an arm and we shook hands. "You're Finchy's volunteer."

I nodded. That's all I'd been. Gabriel's volunteer.

I sat down next to him. "Can I ask you a question?"

"Shoot."

"How did Gabriel get his scar?"

"Knife fight. Ali won."

"I thought they were friends."

"Finchy called him a coward for not marrying Nasreen. One night they had it out. In my opinion, Finchy let Ali crush him so the guys would respect Ali. He still listened to Finchy and proposed, though." His leg started bouncing up and down, fast. "Don't believe whatever you heard. Their deaths were a straight-up accident. Command told Finchy he did right. I was there. I saw it. He didn't have a clear shot. He'd have had to kill the kid to get to the target. Ali and Nasreen, and the others, that little girl, they died because of Ali's cousin. Not because of us."

He scratched his stubble. Then he pulled a tin of Skoal from his back pocket and slid a wad of tobacco under his lower lip.

"But, you know, since then, some of the guys around here call him a Muslim lover 'cause he never fired. Word got around about how tight he was with the terp. Some guys were pissed he made them look bad in a situation fucked up beyond all repair. Then he comes home and builds that crazy-ass mosaic, and, well, no wonder it got vandalized and he got beat. No wonder."

"How come no one else fired?"

"We weren't ordered to."

"So if you were ordered to stand there and watch someone burn you would?"

"That's how it works."

"That's messed up."

"That's avoiding chaos." Rolo stared into the flames. "We thought we were going over to give the people a democracy," he said. "But it's a catch-22. You kill the bad guys and civilians die." He leaned in closer to the fire. "Thing is … you go on enough missions, you come to see both sides. That cousin's whole fuckin' family died in one of our airstrikes. He lost everything. We saw him as the monster and he saw us as the monster." His voice tensed. "We were supposed to get Ali and Nasreen out. She was a cleaner on base. That was in the conditions of them working for us."

I hadn't been there. I knew nothing.

"He used to give that little girl candy," Rolo added. "Told me she reminded him of his kid sister."

"Are you deploying again?" I asked.

"This winter." He flicked a horsefly off his arm.

I got up to go. "Can I take your picture, Rolo?"

"I'd be honored," he said, and stood and made a cheers with his empty cup.

40

One night, following a particularly long shift that involved a spilt tub of refried beans, I came home to find Mom and Nan on the couch watching coverage of the Middle East wars.

Mom hadn't gone back to New York yet. She was staying at the bungalow and sleeping on the couch, catching up with old friends, and Dad didn't seem to mind.

The newscast showed smoky streets, demolished buildings and burned cars. Our troops had trained Iraqi soldiers to blow up their own cities, to force extremist groups out. Then the reporter outlined the US defense plan to issue more drone strikes.

I couldn't watch. I went into my room and they came in after me and sat down on the bed.

"How can he go back?" I sputtered.

"In his mind he has a job to do," Nan said as she put an arm around me. "If it went wrong the first and second times he'll go out again. And again."

"It's not even our country at war. Nobody wants us there."

"That's a technicality. The good old US of A will always be involved."

"He could have been an artist."

"I don't think that was his intention, sweetheart," Mom said quietly. "I think his mosaic was a way of making peace with whatever happened."

"Our town's in Guinness now," Nan said. "He saved Halo."

"I'm sick of hearing that," I said. "Gabriel didn't save Halo."

"His mosaic did, then," Nan replied. "And he did save you, in a sense. From wasting your time following that ninny to California."

I looked at the acrylic chair in the corner of the room, my dirty clothes draped over it. Only one leg was visible, revealing the petals of half a flower.

"I love him," I told them.

"Oh, Twy. He's seen and done too much," Nan said. "You can't expect him to get over it." She left the room while Mom handed me some Kleenex.

Nan came back with a dusty box, blew on it and wiped it with her sleeve, then placed it on the bed. I took the lid off and dumped the photos out. There were hundreds of them, along with envelopes of negatives and slide boxes.

"I ransacked your room a million times for these," I said.

"False backing. Top shelf."

I picked up some prints.

The first one showed a woman in a bamboo hat, crouching and weeping in a field. She held a decapitated body in her arms, the head on a pole beside her.

The next picture was of bloody babies piled on top of each other, eyes open. The next, blindfolded civilians being tortured by soldiers with pointed sticks and machetes.

I flipped to a shot of half-dressed US soldiers dragging a scalped body through the mud, ears and nose carved off the face. There were photos of naked children and adults in mass graves. And there were shots of bodies burned beyond recognition — Vietnamese or American, you couldn't tell.

Grandpa Wallace had written in pencil on the backs of his prints. I started reading the details. Then I ran into the bathroom and threw up.

Nan came in after me. I rinsed my face with cold water before turning to her.

"That's a month's worth from before I even knew him. If you haven't seen enough I have twenty more boxes."

"This is different. What Grandpa saw, where he went, was brutal. These wars aren't Vietnam."

"Because the deed's not personal when it's done by computers, drones and missiles?" Nan asked as I followed her back into the bedroom. "Marines are on the ground. They witness the worst of it. And a war's a war. There's no one war easier than another."

"Were you happy with Gramps?" I asked, my mouth dry.

She gathered the photos, put them back in the box and closed the lid.

"I stood by him. He was too haunted for us to be happy."

I went into the kitchen to do the dishes and Mom and Nan came to help.

After a few minutes, Mom cleared her throat. "I'm sticking around, Twy."

"I'll be fine, Mom."

"I mean I'm moving back."

"What the hell for?"

"Your father and I have decided to try again." I could tell by Nan's face that she already knew. "With all these tourists, I'm thinking I can open a juice bar on Main."

"You told me I could stay with you." I was hit with a sinking feeling. "What am I supposed to do now? Where am I supposed to go?"

"You'll figure it out."

Nan took some keys from her pocket and threw them across the kitchen.

"Now that Halo's not shutting down, I'm happy staying put a little longer," she told me as I caught them.

"I'm not taking the Airstream, Nan," I said, my voice wobbling.

"It's a loan. I'll track you down in a year and head out on my road trip from there. Course I'll need to give you lessons on how to handle her."

Dad was at the door then. "Consider it your ticket outta here. That's what you're angling for, right?"

So they were all in on it. It was official. Nobody in Halo wanted me anymore.

41

I finished the summer out at Taco John's. I gave my room to
Mom, since she and Dad were still working things out on a
trial basis and she wanted her own space.

I packed the Leica and my Rolleiflex, and as many rolls of
film and solutions as I could. And I packed the rose chair.

My family stood outside the bungalow and watched me go.

"You'll be back," Dad said. Then he handed me a box containing a pair of purple boots identical to the ones on my feet.
"For when the originals are too worn out," he told me.

Mom passed me a wad of cash. "Don't talk to strangers.
Keep that camper door locked at night," she said.

I hugged Nan last.

"He-who-shall-not-be-named asked that I put the prize
money into your account," she said.

I felt a tourniquet tightening in my chest.

"Give it to Dad for gambling," I replied.

"I copied my Leonard Cohen albums for you," she added,
ignoring me. "They're in the glove compartment. And I'm not
forgetting about college, missy. We have a deal. You've got one
year." She squeezed me in her arms and wrapped her Slanket
around me. She had to peel me off her and push me into the
Airstream.

As I drove away, my family got smaller in the rearview mirror, until Ash Crescent vanished.

Long after I turned the corner I still pictured them waving at me. Waving, waving goodbye.

I couldn't leave without seeing Trav and Carm one last time, which meant going back to the farm. I hadn't been there in months.

There was a fancier sign at the gate.

Halo Mosaic, it read. *Tour Starts Here.* I passed a long line-up, as Carlos and Hector waved me through.

The mosaic was famous. Divisions of the armed forces arrived by bus, and seniors' travel tours came from all over North America. Tours that used to bypass Halo made a point of adding the silo to their itinerary. And groups from Europe and Asia already had bookings through to the following summer.

There were even special packages that, along with the mosaic tour, included visits to the Angstrom Museum, which stayed open even with the base closed down, lunch at the Sip 'n Sea, and drive-bys of active nuke sites.

The military was involved peripherally, making sure that each visitor setting foot in the silo signed liability papers, saying they were entering at their own risk. This made visitors want to see the mosaic even more.

Someone had built a pebbled path from the farmhouse to the silo. Next to it, I could still see Gabriel's pale ribbon of a trail. And there were sunflowers scattered in the fields, their yellow heads as big as pies.

Trav and Carm came outside with Storm. The dog jumped on me, as obnoxious as ever. Carm showed me her ring, invited me to their wedding and filled my arms with tortilla soup and flautas.

"Walk with me," Travis said, and he went in the direction of the silo.

I knew they'd somehow gotten Gabriel to agree to their "Save the Mosaic" campaign, and had put together enough of a down payment to secure a bank loan and buy the farm outright from the Finches. I'd read about the online fundraiser in the *Interceptor* and I'd seen the donation box at the gate.

Twenty feet before the entryway, there were thick ropes on either side of the path to keep visitors in line.

"No one's in there, Twills," Travis told me, pulling the blast door open. "Heck, they can wait."

He thought I wanted one last visit.

"That's okay," I said, stepping back.

"Take a few minutes," he urged. "I'll be here." He plucked a blade of grass and put it in his mouth and settled onto the bench that had been installed where I'd once sat on a crate watching Gabriel eat an MRE.

The ramp down wasn't dark anymore. There was new lighting like the lights lining the inside of an airplane, and arrows showing the direction to follow. The control room was behind plexiglass with explanatory panels.

But the dome was exactly as Gabriel and I had left it the last time we'd been in there together.

The mosaic still took my breath away. I walked around the circumference, running my hand along the cold metals. I approached the lovers, Ali and Nasreen, where spray paint was still visible on the ammo, like traces of a rare pigment. Gabriel had brought them to the paradise city that Ali had described.

I sat in the middle of the space, lay on my back and looked

up. But without Gabriel there with me, all I was left with was this stabbing ache, urging me to be on my way.

I slowly walked back to the farmhouse with Travis. The sun was warm and grasshoppers jumped all around us.

"I don't even know where I'm going," I told him.

"Just pick a road," he said. "He's deploying soon."

"Why are you telling me this?"

"In case you pick that road."

I wound up on the highway to Fort Stelan. I told myself I'd pass the base and keep going.

Once there, though, I slowed to see infantry units performing outdoor drills and exercises in the field. I drove into the parking lot outside the perimeter to watch them.

But I couldn't see Gabriel among the identical physical training uniforms and synchronized movements. So after an hour I climbed the ladder at the back of the Airstream and stood on top.

By then two officers were approaching. As they came across the parking lot I did the only thing I could think of. I pulled Mom's whistle from under my T-shirt and I blew on it with all the breath left in me. I also hollered his name at the top of my lungs, before the officers insisted I come down and state the nature of my business.

When they began questioning me, I heard his voice.

"It's all right, guys."

I turned and there he was in that same green tracksuit that everyone else in the field wore.

"Hi," he said. I felt like I was looking at a complete stranger.

"Hi," I said back.

"Travis told me you were leaving."

"Yeah."

"Where to?" he asked.

"Not sure yet."

"I'm glad for you, Twyla." Hearing him say my name hurt. He gestured at the motorhome. "Grad gift?"

"I'm just borrowing it."

He glanced at the chair through the window. "You name it yet? The Airstream?"

"Not yet." I hesitated. "Feel like going for a ride?"

"Sure," he said. Then he looked out at the troops in the field. "Give me a sec."

He jogged to the fence and called an officer over. He pointed at me and they spoke.

This was his life now. He couldn't do anything without asking permission anymore.

A few minutes later he climbed in.

"Where to?" I asked as I pulled out of the lot.

"Take a left."

He indicated a turn up the road. I followed his directions, driving another twenty minutes until we arrived at Last Mountain River.

I grabbed a blanket and some lemonade. We found a spot where the water was shallow enough to wade in.

Gabriel pulled off his runners and socks. He dipped one foot in, then the other, as I laid out the blanket. Then we sat looking at the snowless gray-pink Rockies, which appeared mystical, like some distant land we couldn't reach.

We held our knees up, our skin barely touching. When he picked up some rocks I noticed that the casing cuts had disappeared from his fingers.

"How are your parents taking this?" I finally said.

"Dad says it's God's will. Mom's not talking to me."

"I know it was Jeremy and Billy who beat you up," I told him. "That's why you didn't report it. Because it was Billy."

"I had it coming," he said and turned to me. "I did steal his girl."

I looked at his scar and wanted to touch his face.

"Rolo told me what happened," I said. "How there was nothing ... you could have done."

He looked away and skipped a rock across the water.

"You can help the cause from here," I begged. "They need teams to focus on the attacks on domestic ground, don't they?"

"That's not the root of the problem," he said softly. He kept skipping rocks.

"Is it to see Uruk again? I'll go with you someday."

He gave a laugh and caught my eye.

"Come with me," I told him. "There's lots of room. We'll go now. Anywhere you want."

"I'd like that," he said. "Maybe another time."

I looked out at the river, then, and I let myself cry.

Later, we lay on the blanket. As we listened to the sound of the rippling water and the meadowlarks, the sun shining on us, he took my hand.

I turned onto my side to face him, and he turned to face me.

"Before I met you, Twyla, I thought ..."

"What?"

"I thought my heart was a tooth," he said.

"A tooth?"

"Calcified. The nerve buried too deep to feel."

"You've obviously never had a root canal."

"I'm paying you a compliment."

"Worst romantic metaphor I've ever heard, but thanks."

He leaned in at the same time I did, and we kissed.

There was no one around for miles. We had Last Mountain River to ourselves. I pulled my boots, T-shirt and jeans off, and he removed his training uniform.

It was awkward and he seemed as nervous as I was, until everything felt natural, and right, and the pain felt right.

We lay there afterwards for a long time, in each other's arms. It felt to me like we were the last two people in the world.

All my life had been leading up to this place with Gabriel, and it wouldn't have mattered if we died then.

42

Autumn sunups and sundowns in Montana are like nothing else on earth. The infinite purplish sky hints that there's something greater than you out there, and there's nothing you can do about it.

It took me another day to leave the state. I chose a random road east, through the Great Plains where hundreds of nuclear missiles lay beneath our golden fields. Fields that gave off the illusion of forever.

Once in a while a plane flew overhead. Whenever I recognized a gray carrier aircraft through my enormous windshield, I wondered if it was the one taking Gabriel away.

I stopped in at a hardware store and bought paint and a brush and a ruler. That evening at a rest area, I carefully added three words to the side of the motorhome: *Last Mountain River*. Then I sat outside and watched the moon grow dim, thinking how our time together was like a shooting star, brightest as it's about to expire.

For months I zigzagged across the country.

At the end of each day at whatever campground, I built a fire and read from the *Epic of Gilgamesh* until I had the story down by heart. *I will mourn as long as I breathe.* I got a tattoo of this at some point during my travels. Below my breastbone, along a rib.

We wrote a lot at first. The last time we talked I was in Tennessee and I told him I'd hit Graceland for him, and he asked me to buy him an Elvis coffee mug. He'd been there over six months by then.

He spoke of splintered nights, and how he'd finally heard the desert sands sing.

Then he went dark. I had no news.

Rolo was the one who called. He was on a field phone that kept cracking up.

All I understood was that he'd been repairing potholes. Nothing glorious. He didn't save anyone or rescue a little kid.

A few of them were doing roadwork so civilians and supplies could pass, and one of the guys stepped on a wire under gravel that triggered the blast.

Like in his dream, probably.

The city has been my base for a long time now.

I live within walking distance from MoMA and Central Park. Even though I'm barely there.

Instead I find myself traveling to towns like my hometown, taking pictures of enlistees about to serve our country, and those who've returned from serving.

I photograph the before wars and the after wars.

Occasionally I'll go into the darkroom and print a roll picked randomly from a box, and a young, serious face emerges. Sometimes a finger of mine is in the frame, or a wisp of my hair. I find it hard to believe that we were that close together, just a few feet apart. That he was there with me, alive and breathing.

I went home again last year. After meeting up with my parents in Alberta to spread Nan's ashes. There was a letter waiting for me in the bungalow. Mom said it had arrived in the mail the month before.

By then our region was Montana's main destination, with silos turned into subterranean hotels, restaurants and museums. Tourists could see ten in a day, and the Sip 'n Sea was boarded up for demolition.

In the fields surrounding Halo nowadays, there are mosaics made from dog tags and Ripped Fuel, aiming lasers and Kevlars, compasses and signaling mirrors, machine guns, Ka-Bar knives and fire-resistant gloves. I've even heard of one mosaic where members of the Forces can admit to something anonymously, then paste their confession on the wall.

In the deep darkness beneath the earth, some sites are used for prayer, vigils and PTSD meetings. Concerts are held in the old nuclear facilities, too. People come from all parts to experience the music and choirs and children singing.

While there, I stopped in on Trav and Carm.

They'd converted the farm into a Guinness World Records attraction stop and a petting zoo. They were paying off the mortgage and owned the land proper as a registered business, and both their boys told me they wanted to be soldiers.

When I visited them I didn't go down into the silo. But after telling my friends goodbye I did take a walk on the grounds, once the site had closed for the day.

The path he ran was grown over with weeds. His dog was long gone. And the bullet tree had been chopped down.

What remained was a local legend. About a Marine who came home from the wars which still rage on, to make a mosaic from ammunition. Then he went back to those wars and died there.

Another part of the legend was that he fell for a girl from town who helped him with his project. They traveled to New York together where, for one night, he was known as a great artist. He gave her a chair with roses in it, which she treasured.

And their love would endure until the day that rockets hailed from the sky in a silver storm, extinguishing the sun.

A LETTER TO MYSELF

To Me,

If there are still seasons, you're lucky. If there's still a world, you're lucky.

You'll never know his top three songs or movies. His top three candy bars or his favorite flowers. You won't see Paris as a couple.

Hopefully the tall prairie grasses are still here. The rivers and the mountains.

Soon it's going to be Veterans Day again. There'll be wars and wars and wars.

Take in the air and the light, the smells and sounds, then the silence. Take in one last kiss if you can.

Take in this still life.

Nina Berkhout's debut adult novel, *The Gallery of Lost Species*, was highly acclaimed by the *Toronto Star* ("Berkhout does a masterful job") and the *Globe and Mail* ("deeply moving"). The novel was named an Indigo and Kobo Best Book, and a *Harper's Bazaar* Hottest Breakout Novel. She is also the author of five poetry collections. Originally from Alberta, she now lives in Ontario.